MW00943653

Unspoken

This is a work of fiction. Names, characters, places, and incidents either are the product of the author's imagination or are used fictitiously. Any resemblance to actual persons, living or dead, events, or locales is entirely coincidental.

Text copyright © 2019 by Stephanie Dethlefs
Cover art and illustration copyright © 2019 by Gabriella Gonzalez-Yoxtheimer

All rights reserved. Published in the United States by Stephanie Dethlefs.

Visit the website!   unspokenthebook.com

Library of Congress 2019904578

ISBN-13: 978-0-578-49913-0

The text of this book is set in Times New Roman and Ink Free

Printed in the United States of America.

First Edition

UNSPOKEN

by Stephanie Dethlefs

For Eva and Jacob
You are exactly who you are meant to be.

Sometimes a voice says everything, while sometimes it says nothing at all.

Willa G. Vaughn

SEPTEMBER

Day One

"It'll be fine, Sam," said Mom. She put her hand on my shoulder. I pulled away from her and slumped lower in the passenger seat.

We sat across the street from Brooks Middle School. Kids swarmed into the brick building, most in stiff coats and sweatshirts with a few summer holdouts still sporting shorts. Some tumbled out of buses, others jammed bikes into metal racks.

And I didn't know a single one of them.

It wasn't all Mom's fault that we'd moved, that I'd had to change schools a month after seventh grade started. But it was so unfair.

"I'm so glad I have you, honey. You have been the steady one through all of this." I put my hand on the door handle. I felt like I was going to puke.

"I'll see you after I get home from work. I'll bring home some dinner. Marcus will get home from the high school about an hour after you. Remember, walk straight home," she said. Then she sighed. "I love you, kiddo."

"Love you too," I grunted. It sounded more like *lyatoo*.

Mom spoke quietly. "Thanks for under-standing that this is just the way things have to be."

"Yeah." I pushed the car door open and climbed out.

"Have a great day!" she said too cheerfully as I swung the door shut.

Right.

I crossed the street and joined the stream of kids. A girl stopped right in front of me, her head bent over her phone, thumbs tapping the screen, face hidden behind her long hair. I sighed, stepped around her, and made my way into my new reality.

Good morning! I'm sorry I was gone when you got up today. I had an early meeting. You good?

yeah

I'll be home for dinner. Dad's making tacos. Will you remind Jack to feed the cat? He keeps forgetting.

K

I love you Willa. Have a good day, okay?

Love you too Mom

Maybe smile and make some eye contact.

I can sense your sarcasm.

Bye Mom 🖤

Bye Willa 🤍

Welcome to Brooks

I walked up the steps and caught the heavy door before it closed. Inside, the entryway was wide with a large skylight in the ceiling. Kids moved in every direction, their loud voices merging with clicking combination locks and slamming metal locker doors in a deafening ruckus. To my left I saw the sign for the main office, so I dodged the foot traffic and made my way there. When the glass door closed behind me, the noise from the hallway was muted by the thick brown carpet.

The secretary sat behind a desk, digging through a drawer. I cleared my throat.

"Can I help you?" she asked without looking up.

"Um, I'm new," I mumbled.

Her head snapped up and a cheerful smile spread across her broad face, as if this was the best news she'd heard.

"Well, welcome to Brooks!" She slammed her drawer shut and stood up, maneuvering her large body out from behind the desk and over to the counter where I stood. "What's your name?"

"Sam Ward."

"Sam Ward, let's get you going." Her fingers clicked against the keys on her computer. "Locker number 314." She wrote the combination on a card and pushed it across the counter without looking at me. I shoved it in my jeans pocket. "Looks like you are starting the day with Ms. Abaroa in Language Arts, Room 35, then to math with Mr. Wheadon. They can help you figure out where to go next. Give me a minute while I print this schedule out for you."

Math was my strong subject. I liked how numbers fit together like a puzzle. But Language Arts was another story. Of course it made some sick sense that my worst subject would be where I start at this school.

She thrust a paper at me, still warm from the printer. "Room 35, down the hall and to the right," the woman said. "Off you go!" I started a slow shuffle out the door. "Have a lovely day!" she said a little louder, as if her words could physically push me out the door.

The hallway beyond the office was narrow and filled with kids laughing and talking. One wall was lined with two rows of small blue lockers, and I realized that the lady in the office didn't tell me where mine might be. I squinted at one as I passed it: number 107. I sighed. It could take me all day just to find it, let alone the fact that I can never open a combination lock the first time. Someone bumped me and my shoulder slammed into the wall.

"Sorry," he said over his shoulder.

I felt sweat forming on my forehead and upper lip. I came to an intersection and turned right, next to a poster that screamed *Be yourself! No one is better qualified.*

The crowd of kids thinned out and I could finally see where I was going. Room 35 was at the end. I paused and took a deep breath.

Spotlight

The bell rang and I ducked in the door. Keeping my head down, I peeked to find an open chair and was relieved to see one in the back corner. I dropped into it without making a sound as someone laughed. *Keep your head up!* I heard my older brother Marcus say in my head. I wanted to tell invisible Marcus to shove it.

"Good morning, everyone!" chirped a voice from the front. As kids began to sit, they revealed a tiny young woman standing by the white board. She had an enormous grin, golden-brown skin, and freckles. She looked too young to be a teacher. More like she should be working at an ice cream shop.

"Morning, Ms. Abaroa," mumbled a handful of kids. The rest ignored her.

"Okay, attendance. Ashley?"

"Here."

"Jose?"

"Yup."

And so on, until the inevitable moment when the spotlight was on me. "Ah, our new student! Sam?"

"Here."

Twenty faces turned to look at me. My face got hot and my muscles tensed. She tilted her head and looked at me.

"Welcome to Brooks, Sam." She grinned again and moved on.

"Willa?" Silence.

Ms. Abaroa looked up from her computer. "Willa's here," she murmured to herself.

Twenty faces turned to look at the other back corner. A girl sat hunched over her desk, focused on the notebook in front of her. I couldn't tell from where I was sitting if she was writing or drawing.

"She's so weird," I heard the girl named Ashley loud-whisper as she flipped her hair over her shoulder. That's what Marcus calls it when you whisper with full knowledge that everyone will hear it. He used to do that around Dad, trying to get a rise out of him.

Ms. Abaroa studied Willa for a minute, chewing her bottom lip. Then she moved on.

"Xavier?"

"Here."

I passed the time casually glancing at Willa, the girl in the corner. I couldn't see her face through the curtain of brown hair. Her pencil never left the notebook. A couple of times her other hand reached up and rubbed her cheek or nose. Her feet were crossed at the ankles under her desk, clad in purple high top Converse shoes. Her left foot twitched a little. Every other part of her was as still as a statue.

"Okay, my friends, today we are going to start with a quick check-in with our reading partners. Find each other and talk for a couple of minutes about the book you are reading at home." A few soft groans floated through the air as kids stood up and shuffled around the room, finding their partners and sitting back down. I stayed in my seat. So did Willa.

Ms. Abaroa met my eye and held up a finger, telling me silently to wait a minute. She walked over to Willa and murmured something that I couldn't hear. I saw Willa nod, barely. Then Ms. Abaroa made her way over to me and sat down in the vacant seat right in front of me.

"Hi, Sam. How's your first day going?" She looked about the same age as my cousin in college, and she was pretty. My face flushed and I looked at my desk, mortified.

"Good, I guess." I mumbled.

"It's not easy to come to a new school. If you need anything at all just come see me, okay?"

I nodded. Teachers always say stuff like that. Does anyone ever actually do it?

She lowered her voice as if letting me in on a secret. "I'm new here, too. It's an intimidating place. We'll find our way."

I looked up at her. She winked at me and stood. It had become clear by the noise level that no one was talking about their books.

"Alright, everyone. Back to your seats," Ms. Abaroa said loudly. Two boys laughed and high-fived while Ashley and her friend covered their open mouths with their hands, eyes wide in shock. I didn't buy their horror for a second, especially once they started giggling.

"Let's go! Everyone back to your seats!" Ms. Abaroa repeated. Kids began to move with no urgency. Conversations continued.

"You going to practice tonight?"

"Did you hear about James?"

"What IS that? Gross!"

I looked over at Willa. She had stopped writing but was still looking down at her notebook. Her long hair almost touched the top of her desk.

The rest of class passed without much incident. And then Ms. Abaroa assigned homework. "I want everyone to read at least a chapter from their independent reading book tonight," she said. "Pay close attention to the descriptive language. Tomorrow you and your partner will discuss your author's word choice. As we move into our poetry unit this month, we are going to explore how words evoke feelings in the reader."

I sighed. Words on a page were my nemesis. They floated around, mixing themselves up like Scrabble tiles, only instead of arranging themselves into words that made sense they did the opposite, and left me no way to decipher them.

Back in elementary school, when I had to read out loud to my teachers, it was harder. I would point at it, forcing that first letter to stay in the right place, squint my eyes and say that letter's sound two or three times. Eventually the teacher would tell me the word and we would move on to the next one. As soon as I was told to read to myself, I would pick up a book I had heard before, or one with a lot of pictures.

The trick to talking about books without reading them is being a good listener. Teachers always read aloud, and I pay attention. As I walked out of language arts, I thought back on my list of familiar titles, settling on

Hatchet, which my fifth grade teacher read aloud. I remembered enough of it that I could refer to it for days if needed.

"Hey," someone said, grabbing my arm from behind. I turned around. It was the loud-whisperer, Ashley. She was standing with another girl. "What's your name again?" she asked.

"Uh, Sam," I said, sounding like the dumbest person around. Both girls were really pretty, with makeup and long hair and that funny way of blinking that some girls have.

"Hi, Uh Sam," she said, holding out a hand to shake mine vigorously. Her friend giggled behind her binder. "I'm Ashley." She dropped my hand and started to walk away. "See you around, Uh Sam!" she said loudly over her shoulder. Then she and her friend laughed as they walked away.

I hate girls sometimes. I looked at the lockers outside Ms. Abaroa's room. The numbers ranged upward from 175. I started walking, keeping my eyes on the numbers of the lockers. I wasn't even close to where I needed to be.

When I was ten,
a boy in my class
– Jason –
told everyone that
I was
dumb.

When the teacher
heard about it, he said
– with a smirk –
that he meant
dumb as in
can't talk

Which is old-fashioned
and rude
and just as bad
if you ask me

The teacher said
"Apologize to Willa."
He did,
– didn't mean it, though –
and my voice burrowed
deeper
into its hole
way down
inside me.

Willa G. Vaughn

I can talk fine.

It's just when I'm

        scared
      nervous
     sad
      worried
        angry
          anxious
            frustrated
        happy
       excited
     surprised
      skeptical
        confused
         lonely

my voice gets stuck
behind a wall
a bit too high
for it to see over
to know for sure
that it's safe
to come out.

Willa G. Vaughn

14

Half Points

Second period was math. I wound my way there, eyeing lockers on the way and noticing that the numbers were getting higher. I still hadn't spotted number 314, but I was getting closer.

I stepped into the classroom and looked around for an open seat. There was one—right in the front row center. I sat down and was pretending to look for something in my binder when the teacher walked in.

To say this guy was a mess is an understatement. His clothes were wrinkled, like he'd slept in them or left them in a pile on the floor. Wisps of graying hair stood on end and his glasses were crooked. He dropped his armload of folders and papers on his desk and sat down behind it. When he looked out into the class, his eyes landed on me first.

"Well, you're new," he said.

I stared at him. "Yes sir," I mumbled.

"Didn't know I was getting a new student. Okay then, let's get this ball rolling. Homework out, please."

The students around me didn't speak as they dug into their bags. This wrinkled little man had some sort of power over them. At my old school, kids would have eaten this guy for breakfast. But here they quietly set their papers on their desks and didn't speak.

"Who's first?" Mr. Wheadon asked.

I heard the rustle of hands shooting up into the air.

"Jones."

A girl's voice rose from the back of the room. "I found problem 12 especially challenging because there were multiple strategies I could have used, and I wasn't sure what the best one would be."

Mr. Wheadon wrote a note.

"Good. Next?" Hands went up again. "Martinez."

The boy next to me spoke. "The last problem was fun because it was challenging but in a good way."

Mr. Wheadon looked at the boy. "Half points. I want to hear specifics. Next?" Hands went up again.

This system went on for the entire class period. Students reported their thinking about one problem on the homework, and Mr. Wheadon responded with "Good" or "Half points." Since I didn't have a math book or the homework, I had no idea what kind of math they were even talking about. When I'd left my old school, we'd just started an algebra unit and a group project. I felt pretty confident I'd be able to do whatever it was that was happening here.

When the bell rang, no one moved. Mr. Wheadon opened his math textbook and flipped through the pages. Finally he spoke. "Pages 35 and 36. Turn in your work on your way out, please."

Everyone rose and filed past his desk, each setting his or her paper in a neat pile on the corner. I waited until everyone had gone by before standing.

"You," Mr. Wheadon said. "What's your name?"

"Sam Ward."

"Okay," he said. Then he reached behind his chair to the bookshelf behind him. "Do your homework. Extra credit points are given for participation."

I took the thick textbook from his outstretched hands and nodded. He pulled the pile of papers on the corner of his desk toward him, picked up a red pen, and got to work. I slipped out of the room.

Shaking my head, I thought about how I would explain that guy to Marcus. I decided to let it go for now. A more pressing issue was the weight of the math book, which I really didn't want to carry around. I looked at the lockers outside Mr. Wheadon's room. Number 300! If nothing else, I would find my stupid locker.

The perks of not talking?
  Hearing.
  Seeing.
I'm like a tiny spider on the wall.
  Listening,
  Watching,
Barely visible to anyone.

                         Willa G. Vaughn

Home Not Home

The apartment was on the same street as the school, with exactly ten and a half blocks between them. In between were a strip mall, a skate park, a library, an empty lot with dumpsters overflowing, and a bank. I turned into our apartment complex. Three buildings sat in a U-shape around a courtyard with a dry fountain in the middle. I walked up the uneven brick path to our door on the first floor of the middle building.

My stomach rumbled. I had opted out of the cafeteria today—it's the worst for a new kid. Where do you sit? Who do you sit with? I couldn't handle it, so I spent most of lunch break in a bathroom stall, and never got anything to eat. I hoped there was something good in the fridge.

I had survived the first day of school in a town that wasn't home, with kids I'd never seen before.

When I'd moved up to middle school in sixth grade, at least there had been some familiar faces from elementary school, including my friend Chris. He and I ate lunch together every day and hung out on the weekends. I slept over at his house and we played video games late into the night. He is the only person I told about Dad.

I shook my head, trying to shake the thought right out of my mind the way a dog shakes off water. I reached up to adjust my baseball cap. There was too much to get used to here, and if I started thinking about Dad…well, I just wasn't going to go there.

We'd moved to this town a week earlier, in the middle of the day while Dad was gone. Mom had already rented the apartment and bought a cheap couch, coffee table and TV for the living room and beds for the bedrooms. There were two bedrooms, one for Mom and one for me and Marcus to share. The look on her face when she told us we'd be sharing a room warned us there would be no grumbling about it, and Marcus elbowed me in the ribs before I could complain. The two twin beds took up most of the room. Marcus grinned and flopped on the one closest to the window. "Dibs!" he shouted.

"Hey, man!"

I turned to look at our neighbor, an old man named Gus who sat outside his door on a plastic lawn chair every day. He always had a newspaper folded up in his lap, but never seemed to be reading it.

"Hi, Gus," I replied, digging into my pocket for my house key. "How's it going?"

"Goin' good, can't complain!" he grinned. I noticed he was missing a tooth. "You rootin' for the Bells?" He pointed at my cap.

"Um, nah, this hat is old," I mumbled, deciding not to tell Gus that Dad took me and Marcus to almost every home game last year.

"How's your mama? Such a nice lady."

I was pretty sure Gus had a crush on my mom, which I found a little creepy but harmless. He asked about her every day. "She's fine, Gus. I'll see you later."

"See you later, my man. See you later." He started whistling as I pushed through our front door.

After slapping together a PB&J sandwich, I headed straight for the couch, flopping down and grabbing the remote. I flipped channels until I landed on Judge Judy's court show. Judge Judy told it like it was. Judge Judy didn't let anyone get away with stupid stuff. I wondered what Judge Judy would have to say about our current situation. I drifted into a fantasy where Mom was at one podium, Dad at the other. Judge Judy looked sympathetically at Mom and wagged her finger at Dad. Then she stated her verdict, and her gavel pounded the wood.

And kept pounding.

Alternatives

As I slowly woke up, I realized that the sound wasn't Judge Judy's gavel pounding, it was pounding on our front door. I sat up, wiped a stream of drool from my cheek, and went to open it.

"Dude, what took you so long?" Marcus breezed into the apartment, filling it up with his five-foot-ten frame and his boisterous energy. He dropped his backpack next to mine on the floor.

"Where's your key?" I asked. My head was still fuzzy from sleep.

"Dunno," he said. "I'm hoping it's in my pants from yesterday." He flopped on the couch and picked up the remote, flipping the channel to a baseball playoff game.

"Nuh-uh, I was watching that!" I said, trying to grab the remote from his hand.

"Snooze you lose, brother," he said. "And from the look of that crease on your face, you've been snoozing a while."

I sat on the couch next to him. Truthfully, I didn't care what we watched. I just liked being around Marcus. Something about his attitude always reassured me that everything was going to okay, even when it wasn't.

Marcus is the exact opposite of me in practically every way. He's tall and handsome while I'm skinny and kind of goofy-looking. He's good at everything and crazy popular wherever he goes. I was sure that after one day he was already friends with everyone at the high school. The only conversations I'd had that day were with teachers, plus that one with a girl I'd rather forget about.

Not that Marcus didn't get mad sometimes; there had been times where I expected smoke to come out of his ears. He'd grit his teeth, flare his nostrils, and get so quiet that backing away seemed like the smart option. But when he was in a good mood, there was no one else I'd rather hang around with.

Marcus punched me in the arm. "Got homework, little man?"

I punched him back. "Shut up," I retorted. "I'm almost as tall as you."

"Yeah, but who's better looking?" he asked, puffing out his chest and looking down his nose at me. "Seriously, got homework? I have some math I gotta do. Mom'll want us to do it before she gets home."

I looked at him skeptically. "Who made you the boss?"

"Might as well be me," he grunted as he pressed himself up from the couch. "Beats the alternative."

"Oh, yeah?" I said. "What's the alternative? A person who chills out?" I stayed put on the couch.

Marcus looked at me. "The alternative is Dad."

We stared at each other until I gave in and grabbed my backpack.

Barely visible to anyone,
except Sarah.
She lived next door
for most of my life
and is my best friend.
She knows what I
heard
   saw
      felt
just from the look on my face
or the shrug of my shoulders.

But she moved.

Willa G. Vaughn

Expectations

I sat at the round wooden dining room table with math homework spread out in front of me. I had no intention of reading tonight.

The front door opened. Mom walked in holding white plastic takeout bags in one hand and a bunch of file folders in the other. Her purse dangled from her elbow.

"A little help here, please?" she said, a hint of irritation in her voice. Marcus popped up from where he'd been reading on the couch and took the food from her.

"Hey Mom," I said.

"Hi, kiddo," she replied, pausing on her way to the kitchen to kiss the top of my head. At some point she would have to realize that I'm not a kid anymore, but this wasn't the time to point that out. "I got Chinese."

"Nice!" said Marcus, already in the kitchen and pulling a Styrofoam container out of a bag. "Sweet and Sour!"

"How were your first days of school?" Mom asked as she set down her folders on the table next to me and peeled off her coat. "Sam? You first."

"Fine," I mumbled. There was always this expectation, like I would tell her everything, but the thought of replaying an entire day was too much so I never did. "I have math homework."

"Do you like your teachers?" she asked, sitting in the chair across from me and pulling off her shoes.

I shrugged. "I guess," I said. "Don't really know yet."

She leaned back in the chair and stared off somewhere to my right. Her eyes seemed to glaze over for a minute. They looked puffy, like she hadn't slept in days. I guessed she probably hadn't. Then she shook her head and her eyes came back into focus.

"Marcus? How 'bout you?"

Over dinner, Marcus told us about how the drummers from the marching band banged on their instruments in the hallway to hype people up for the weekend's football game. Mom talked about spotting a bowling alley across town on her way home from work and suggested maybe we go over the weekend. They teased each other and me, trying to get me to open up about my day, but I had nothing to say about it.

After a moment of quiet chewing, Mom spoke again.

"You guys will be okay here, right?"

Marcus grunted an "uh-huh" and I shrugged, pushing chow mein noodles around on my plate.

"I know this is hard. It's hard for me, too. But it's what we have to do right now," she said, setting her fork down and leaning back in her chair. I could tell that she *needed* us to say it was okay, but I wasn't sure it was.

"Have you talked to Dad?" I asked. The question came out of my mouth before I realized I was wondering it. Marcus kicked me under the table.

"No, I haven't," she said. "I'm not ready yet."

"Does he know where we are?" I asked. Why was I asking these questions? Mom had told us we would talk about it when there was something new to discuss.

"Cut it out!" Marcus hissed. He had become increasingly protective of Mom in recent weeks.

"Marcus, it's okay," Mom sighed, rubbing her forehead with both hands before sliding her fingers down her face. "Yes, he knows where we are. I told him not to contact us, that I would call him when I was ready to talk. If." That last word sent a chill down my back. *If* she's ready? Like she might not ever be ready?

"Mom, we'll do dishes," Marcus said, already rising to clear the table. "You just relax."

"Thanks, hon," she said. "I think I need a hot shower." She walked to the bathroom and shut the door.

I rinsed the dishes and Marcus put them in the dishwasher without a word. I could see his jaw muscles flexing under his cheek, so I knew he was mad at me. Or just mad in general. I opted not to push.

Closing the dishwasher, Marcus turned to face me. "Dude, you have to back off of her," he said quietly. "We don't need to make anything worse than it already is." He brushed past me and walked into the living room.

I stood leaning back against the sink, staring at the fading yellow flower wallpaper and dark wood paneling on the wall. I had more questions than answers, but it didn't look like I was getting any answers soon.

I crossed through the apartment without making a sound and shut our bedroom door. I needed something from my old life. Reaching under my bed, I slid the dark green guitar case out and popped it open. I ran my fingers across the body and onto the strings, plucking each one just once.

Basics

Dad had given me this guitar for my tenth birthday, after he'd found it at a second-hand shop and tuned it up. He said he thought it would be a good fit for me, and he was right. He showed me the basics.

"The basics are all I've got, my friend!" he'd laughed in his booming way, like it erupted from deep in his center. After that, I devoured everything I could find online and taught myself how to play a few simple pieces.

The melody of a new song had come to me one day when I was walking home from Chris's house. I started humming as I walked, and when I got home it was only a matter of time before I'd plucked it out, added some chords, and had a piece that was all my own. Mom bought me some music paper for writing down the notes. I guess she didn't realize that I couldn't read or write music.

The song did everything for me. If I was down in the dumps, it lifted me up. If I was mad, it calmed me down. It had changed a bit over the past year, but the basics were the same.

The basics were all I needed.

Hi!

Hi Willa girl!

Sorry that I didn't text you yesterday. You have a lot of homework at your new school?

Yes, tons. Science teacher is crazy, too! LOL what's up with you?

Not much. School sucks. I miss you

Miss you too. Hate being the new kid.

At least you can talk to people

You'll find someone else who gets you

Hope so.

Gotta go, talk tomorrow?

Yep!

Morning

Mom knocked on my bedroom door as she opened it, an annoying habit I needed to ask her to stop. I looked back down at my guitar.

"Morning, kiddo," she said. "Sleep well?"

"Yeah," I mumbled, still plucking at the strings.

"Eat breakfast yet?"

"Yeah."

"Do you want a ride today?"

"Nah."

She sighed. "Okay, Mr. Conversationalist," she said, leaning down to kiss the top of my messy hair. "See you tonight. Have a good second day."

"Uh huh," I grunted.

"Love you!" she said as the door clicked shut.

Morning, Last Year

Dad knocked on my door and hollered through. "Can I come in?"

"Yeah!"

"That's a little loud, my friend," he shouted as he entered.

"Sorry," I said, and turned the volume down on my computer. "I'm watching Jimi Hendrix play."

"Whoa, now that's a high standard you are setting for yourself," Dad laughed as he sat on my bed. "Maybe take a few lessons first."

"You know I don't want to, Dad," I replied. "I just like messing around on the guitar."

"I know, but if you take lessons you can go to the next level. Like Jimi there." He gestured at the computer screen.

"He never took lessons."

"Seriously? Huh," Dad said. "Well, kid, listen. You follow your own path. When something feels like the right thing to do, that's what you do." His face fell for a second, and I looked away.

Dad had lost his supervisory job at the construction company. He told us it wasn't a big deal, an "amicable parting of the ways," which I guess meant he wasn't technically fired. But

I could tell it was bothering him, and I didn't know what to say.

"Okay, Dad."

"I mean it. You're a smart person. Trust your gut." He ruffled my hair as he went out of the room. "Do you want a ride to school today?"

"Sure."

"Well, hop to it! This train is leaving the station in five. Got to pound some pavement and find a new job. Today's the day! I can feel it!" His booming voice filled the hallway and entered my room, as though he hadn't just walked out.

Day Two

The bell for the start of Language Arts rang with no sign of Ms. Abaroa. Kids didn't seem to notice. Ashley, the girl who had embarrassed me the day before, leaned across the aisle between desks, whispering to another girl and looking back at me. I pretended to look for something in my binder.

I heard a giggle and suddenly Ashley appeared in the seat in front of me, her long ponytail draped over the back of her chair. This couldn't be good.

Ms. Abaroa fluttered in, her arms loaded with papers and her face flushed. "Sorry, folks," she said, laughing. "Had a disagreement with the copy machine." She set the papers down on her desk and pulled at the bottom of her blouse to straighten it out. "Good morning!"

"Good morning, Ms. Abaroa!" Ashley chirped loudly as the talking in the room ceased. She looked over her shoulder at me and grinned.

Ms. Abaroa nodded her head. "Okay, I'll do attendance while you get started with your homework discussions. Find your reading partners. Remember, you are focusing today on what you noticed about the author's word choice." She had to practically yell this last part because kids had already started talking and moving, their chairs scraping on the lino-leum floor.

Ashley turned around to face me. "What's your name again?" she asked me. Her lips shined with gloss and gum snapped between her teeth. I could feel my brain shrinking. That's what happened to me around girls like Ashley: my brain actually shrunk until I had absolutely nothing to say and looked as dumb as a boulder.

I also felt a hint of fear. Ashley's eyes didn't look kind.

"Sam," I mumbled.

"Right," she grinned. "So, where did you move from?"

"Lyndale," I mumbled again.

"Ooohh," she nodded with approval, as though I had come from some magical king-dom. Her eyes flickered, something secretive bubbling up behind them. "So, Sam from Lyndale, do you…"

"Ashley, what are you doing?" Ms. Abaroa materialized next to us. "Sophia is your read-ing partner."

"I know," Ashley's face changed in an instant. She now looked almost angelic, as though a halo might appear over her head. "But I saw that Sam didn't have a partner yet, and I think we should always include our new students, don't you, Ms. A.?" Her eyes widened, taking over most of her face. She blinked innocently. "I'm sure you would agree."

Ms. Abaroa's forehead crinkled a little, and she pursed her lips as she considered Ashley's comment. "Yes, that's true, Ashley. But why don't you go back to your seat now?"

"Okay, Ms. A." Ashley popped out of her seat and pulled her ponytail over her shoulder. "I was just trying to help." She meandered back up the aisle, stopping to chat with a pair of boys in the front row. She laughed loudly at whatever they said.

Ms. Abaroa touched my arm. "I'm so sorry, Sam, I completely forgot. I'll set you up with a reading partner tomorrow," she said. "You can just read to yourself for a few minutes. Do you have a book?"

"Uh, yeah," I nodded, even though I did not. I opened my binder like I had one tucked in there.

Ms. Abaroa patted my shoulder as she stood and moved over to sit next to the quiet girl in the corner.

Willa. I hadn't noticed her.

Ms. Abaroa sat sideways in the desk next to Willa's with her back to me. I could tell that Ms. Abaroa was saying something, though I couldn't hear it over the conversations of the rest of the class.

Then Willa looked up. Her face turned to Ms. Abaroa. The teacher's head blocked my view of most of Willa's face, but I could see her eyes. They were big and bright, with long dark lashes. They gave off heat, like sun coming through a window.

In an instant her eyes were gone again, hidden behind her hair. Her purple Converse high tops were motionless under her desk.

I was curious about her. Tomorrow, I decided, I would sit closer so that I could hear.

You were my friend,
once
before Jason
decided that calling me
dumb
would make people laugh
        (didn't it?)
and they would like him more
      (didn't they?)
but the worst part was
when you laughed,
deciding at that moment
you were done with me.

Before that we
were three friends

Willa
  Sarah
    Ashley

Now there's just me.

                    Willa G. Vaughn

Prey

The thought of eating in the cafeteria was as intimidating as it had been the day before, but I couldn't hide forever. I found a seat at an empty table closest to the door and inhaled my lunch. When I finished, I tossed my garbage and left the cafeteria, thinking I could kill some time by walking slow, using the bathroom, and getting a drink of water. Then I would only need to spend a few minutes outside by myself before the bell rang for next period.

I turned the corner and saw a familiar ponytail. Ashley was standing outside of the bathrooms with a group of girls, whispering. I felt that strange fear from earlier prickling my spine. If I walked past them, there would be no Ms. Abaroa to intercept us. There was no one else in the hall.

Ashley reminded me of a spider, waiting for someone to get stuck in her web. I really didn't want to be that someone.

The girls' bathroom door swung open, and Willa walked out. With her head down, she cast a glance over her shoulder and, seeing the group of girls on her right, immediately pivoted left and started walking in my direction.

"Hey, Willa!" Ashley called out.

Willa kept walking.

"What's the matter, Willa?" Ashley's voice got louder as Willa walked away, as if her words were trying to chase Willa down the hall. The girls around her giggled, and they all leaned in to whisper again.

Just then an adult I didn't recognize stepped out of a classroom. "Girls, where should you be right now?"

"Sorry, Mr. Hernandez," the cluster of girls murmured in unison as they began to migrate down the hall.

"Bye, Willa!" Ashley yelled over her shoulder. Her voice hit me in the face like a slap.

As Willa got closer her eyes lifted briefly to meet mine. While I thought I might see tears or embarrassment caused by Ashley's taunting, I only saw confidence, her furrowed brow lending a dose of defiance. And then she disappeared into the sea of people in the cafeteria.

American Girl and
rubber band bracelets
lost their place to
makeup and
boys and
gossip and—

We played
games of
imagination and—

When I look
at you now I see
a mask.

The girl that used to
paint by number and
build stuffed animal cities and
whisper to me about her mom's
latest boyfriend and—

You play
games of
manipulation and—

When you look
in mirrors do you see
yourself?

Willa G. Vaughn

44

Bad Days

Mom fluttered around the kitchen like a trapped bird.

"Ugh, this commute is killing me," she muttered. "Not enough time...can't get anything done...where is my *mug*?" She slammed the cupboard door and opened another one.

"Hey, Mom," Marcus said, his mouth full of Cheerios. "Take a breath."

She turned and glared at Marcus for a split second before her gaze softened. "You're right, I'm going nuts." She found her travel mug and tipped the coffee pot over it. Coffee spilled all over the counter and splashed onto her shirt. "FOR THE LOVE OF..." she wailed.

"MOM!" Marcus interrupted, jumping up from his chair. "Relax! I'll clean it up. Go change."

I shook my head as Mom stormed out of the kitchen and Marcus mopped up the coffee with a kitchen towel. Ever since we'd moved to this apartment, Marcus had taken care of Mom as much as she took care of us. Regardless of what mood he was in, he seemed to always know what to say to help her.

I, on the other hand, never knew what to say.

I looked down at my cereal and pushed it around the bowl with the spoon for a minute, before setting it in the sink and leaving the kitchen. Back in our bedroom I picked up my guitar. I leaned back on my bed with my back against the wall and picked at the strings, remembering another time in another kitchen.

About four months had passed since Dad lost his job. To help with the finances, Mom had asked for and gotten more responsibility in her office, which came with both a slight raise and a lot more work. She came home later each night, and tensions were rising between her and Dad.

"You could have at least made dinner," I heard her say, slamming the cupboard doors shut.

Marcus and I were watching TV in the small room off the kitchen.

"I didn't know you wanted me to," he replied. I heard the crack of a beer can opening.

"I shouldn't *have* to ask you," she retorted, her voice rising. "You're home all day. I'm not."

"Oh, here we go," he muttered.

Marcus and I looked at each other. It was an unspoken question every time. Should we leave the room? Intervene? Or try to become invisible?

Fortunately, that fight ended there. They didn't always. Sometimes they went late into the evening, both of them shouting while we hid in our rooms and pretended not to notice.

By contrast, the dinner table was always quiet, Mom or Dad stiffly asking us questions and Marcus and I answering as normally as possible.

I had another flash of memory. Dad leaning in my bedroom door frame with the look of a dog who'd been kicked, holding a beer, just listening as I played.

Another flash of memory. Going to get a drink of water in the middle of the night and seeing Mom and Dad, sitting at the kitchen table holding hands, both of them crying.

First Contact

The next day I walked into Language Arts class and sat down next to Willa. Her head was down and her pencil was moving. I tried to make myself look busy by shuffling my binder around and pulling out a pencil, but mainly I was watching her. As always, she looked like a statue, long hair draped over her face and skimming her arm as she…what *was* she doing? I looked closer but couldn't see through her hair. I leaned forward a little, then a little more, until I could see a small notebook with words scribbled all over it.

"Hi, Sam from Lyndale!" Ashley's voice pierced my brain like lightning.

I jerked up, and as I did my binder and pencil fell on the floor. Laughter bubbled around me as I squatted down on the floor to pick them up. A purple Converse high top pushed my pencil toward me along the floor. I looked up at Willa. She was still writing, but I thought I could see the corners of her mouth lifted into a grin.

"Hey, I didn't mean to *scare* you," Ashley giggled from across the room. "I was just saying hi."

"It's fine," I muttered, rising back up to my seat and settling in.

"You should sit here," she said, patting the empty desk behind her.

"Uh…um…" I stammered. I wanted to sit by Willa, and I didn't want to sit by Ashley, and I wasn't sure why on either count. *No, thanks, I'm good here,* I said in my head, but of course the words didn't leave my mouth.

Fortunately, Ms. Abaroa breezed in. "Good morning, everyone!"

Conversations continued. Ashley looked at me through squinted eyes.

"Good MORNING, everyone!" Ms. Abaroa said, more loudly this time.

"G'morning," a few kids mumbled, and the class began to settle down.

"Alright, you know the drill," she said. "Find your reading partners and reflect on what you read last night while I take attendance."

She said nothing to me about a reading partner, so I stayed where I was and silently prayed Ashley would not come over. I could still hear her voice chasing Willa down the hall yesterday.

I probably should have said something. But what?

"Good morning, Sam," Ms. Abaroa said, materializing beside me. "I'd decided to partner you with Jose, but he's absent today. So how 'bout you chat with Willa and me?"

"Um...'k," I answered. Willa didn't look up, but she closed her notebook and set her pencil beside it.

"Super!" Ms. Abaroa seemed unnecessarily pleased. "Willa, how about you go first?" Willa didn't move. Ms. Abaroa leaned in. "Willa," she whispered. "Look at me."

Willa slowly lifted her eyes until they locked with Ms. Abaroa's. She jutted her chin out just a little, like it was keeping the rest of her head from falling forward again.

"Thank you," said Ms. Abaroa quietly. "Are you still reading *Everything, Everything*?"

Willa nodded.

"What language did Nicola Yoon use that stood out to you?"

Willa glanced down at her notebook. As she opened it I noticed that her fingernails were painted green and orange on alternating fingers. She flipped through some pages and handed the notebook to Ms. Abaroa.

Ms. Abaroa read the page, then smiled. "Great," she said. "Are you enjoying the book?"

Willa nodded. Ms. Abaroa looked at me, and I could feel my face flush.

"I'm actually reading that book too," I lied.

"Really?" Ms. Abaroa looked surprised, but only for a second. "So where did *you* find the author's word choice to be most powerful?" She looked at me steadily, her head tilted.

"Uh…in the part where they are imagining sitting in the restaurant with the astronaut," I blurted.

Ms. Abaroa smiled a gentle smile at me, her freckles squishing up toward her eyes. "Thank you, Sam," she said. "Tomorrow you can partner with Jose." She stood and walked back to the front of the classroom, attempting and failing to get everyone's attention.

I glanced sidelong at Willa. She was looking at me and, almost imperceptibly, shaking her head. I turned to face her.

"What?" I asked.

Her eyes danced and the corners of her mouth lifted into a smirk. She opened her notebook and tore out a page, scribbled something, and handed it to me. I took it from her green and orange fingertips.

That isn't in the book, it's only in the movie.

I looked back at her. Her eyes were laughing, but in a friendly way. For the first time since I'd walked into Brooks Middle School, I relaxed.

Dark hair
curling out from
under a blue cap
like tentacles
waving
as he walks
down the steps.

And I wonder
who is this kid?
And I wonder
why does he
look at me
like I'm a
weird animal
at the zoo?
(Not a cool one)
        Tiger
            Lion
(Not a cute one)
    Arctic fox
    Baby panda
An odd one:
        Aardvark
            Porcupine
Is he trying to figure out
why I'm alone?

And I wonder,
why is HE alone?
Maybe he is an aardvark, too.

Willa G. Vaughn

Seeing Ghosts

After school, my backpack was loaded with books and folders for homework, so full my binder didn't even fit. I moved out onto the front steps, swept along by the wave of hundreds of new schoolmates. It amazed me that I could be surrounded by so many kids and not know anyone.

I reached up to put on my baseball cap and my binder fell out of my hand, landing on the concrete stairs. At least three people kicked it in their rush to get away from the school. By the time I scrambled down the steps to it, the rings had popped open and some papers had flown out. I bent down to gather everything as people pushed past me.

Super. Now I was not only a new kid, but the dorky one who dropped stuff. This day was just getting better and better, I thought.

"Sam!"

I thought I heard my name, but who would be shouting it?

"SAM!"

That time I knew I heard it. A familiar voice that punched me right in the gut. I stood up and looked around.

Dad.

"Sam! C'mere!" he hollered from the sidewalk, waving frantically. "Over here! Sam!"

My feet were stuck. He walked toward me.

"Sam! Hey, bud," he said, his voice lowering as he got closer. "Hi!"

"Um, hi, Dad," I said quietly, looking around. I think I wanted to see Mom, to see if this was okay.

"Let me help you with this," he said, squatting down to gather up the last of my papers and snapping my binder closed. He grunted as he stood up and looked at me again. "Hey, bud," he said again.

"Dad, um, what are you doing here?" I asked. I looked around again. What was I afraid of? There was no rule against him coming to the school. It's fine, I told myself, though I didn't quite believe it.

"I wanted to see my boy. I've missed you," he answered, putting his hand on my shoulder and squeezing it. "Man, I've missed you." He pulled me into an awkward hug.

His wrinkled flannel shirt smelled stale. I pulled back, but he held on, arms wrapped around me. He leaned in to me so much that I was afraid he'd fall if I moved.

"Dad..." I said, pushing harder against his arms. He let go this time. "What do you want?"

"I told you, I just wanted to see you," he said. His smile faded. "Is that so wrong?"

"No, it's just..." my voice trailed off.

He stared at me, and I realized his body was swaying ever so slightly, like a thin tree in a breeze. "Oh, right...okay," he said "Right. I should go." He ran a hand through his thinning hair and then shoved his hands into the pockets of his rumpled jeans. "Right," he said again. "I'll see you, I guess..."

"Dad," I said as he turned to walk down the steps, but he didn't stop. I didn't call out again. I watched him as he walked down the sidewalk in front of the school, then turned the corner. I watched a while longer even though I couldn't see him anymore.

My throat closed around all the words I didn't say, and that I wouldn't say later to Marcus or Mom. I glanced around to see if anyone had seen. There were a few kids left on the steps, including Willa, who was standing a few steps up from me. Our eyes met, but she quickly looked away and ran down the steps toward a line of cars waiting to drive kids home. I started walking toward our apartment, my heart pounding.

In math today
we practiced
ratios.

The ratio of
father to son
looks like

begging : resisting

reaching forward : stepping back

anguish : confusion

afraid : love

love: afraid

Willa G. Vaughn

OCTOBER

Is a friend
a person who
sits with you
at lunch?
Walks with you
down the hall?
Gossips with you
in the bathroom?

If that's the case,
I have none.

Or is it a person who
sits beside you in a single class?
Glances at you
with the furtiveness
of a skittish mouse?
Mutters comments
under his breath while
staring at his desk,
knowing you can hear?

If that's the case,
I have one.

Willa G. Vaughn

61

Unspoken

For two weeks, I sat next to Willa every day. I don't know why, but I really felt like I wanted to talk to her.

Over the past weekend, Marcus told me his theory that if something is totally out of reach, it makes you want it even more. He was talking about our favorite burger place in Lyndale, but it seemed to me the theory applied here, too.

It wasn't just the challenge, though. Willa's facial expressions interested me. Sometimes her mouth curled into a smirk if someone made a dumb joke. Other times I could tell that she was rolling her eyes even though I couldn't see them. She didn't make eye contact very often or for very long, but when she did, I swear I could see what she was thinking.

I know that sounds weird.

Every once in a while, I'd whisper a sarcastic comment under my breath, just loud enough for her to hear. (Like the time Max offered to go make copies for Ms. Abaroa when she'd forgotten, I whispered, "See you at the end of class, Max!") Each time, I'd sneak a sidelong glance at Willa, and would be rewarded with a slight grin or wrinkled nose.

One time, she actually snorted.

I never did get partnered with Jose for reading. I think Ms. Abaroa forgot all about it. But every day Ms. Abaroa sat down in the chair in front of Willa and asked us both about what we were reading. Willa always had her notes ready, but she never spoke.

And she seemed to know that I was always faking. I could tell by the shake of her head, or her *you're kind of an idiot* grin, or the note she would pass me when Ms. Abaroa left.

Didn't you read that book in elementary school? I did.

You should talk about a different book tomorrow. It's been a week.

And so on. But it never felt mean. It felt like she was trying to help me.

Show Up

The headache started during lunch, while I sat at a table with Jose and Max and some of their friends. I'd been eating with them for a week or so, and they were nice enough, but I was always on the outside of the conversation. They threw around inside jokes and made references to things that I didn't know about. I'd started to dread the balancing act of trying to look and sound cool while wishing you were somewhere else.

I made it through the rest of the day with my head pounding, and now all I wanted to do was sleep. After the daily banter with Gus by the front door—each word feeling like a hammer pounding the backs of my eyes—I stumbled into the apartment and almost jumped out of my shoes. Marcus was sitting on the couch, flipping through TV channels.

"There he is! I've been waiting for you!" he said. He patted the couch cushion next to him. "Get over here. I have to show you something."

"Marcus, what are you doing here? Why are you home so early?" I asked.

Marcus flicked the TV off. He pulled a piece of paper out of his back pocket, unfolded it, and slapped it onto the coffee table.

"Check it out," he grinned.

"What is it?" I asked. I was skeptical.

The corners of his mouth turned up in an evil grin. "Look, dummy!" He jabbed at the paper with his finger like he was trying to nail it to the table. "It's your moment of greatness! A chance to play your guitar for people!"

I sat down next to him and leaned forward. The corners of the flyer were torn and the center was crinkled. He'd probably pulled it off a telephone pole. The words swam around the page until finally enough of them settled into place that I could make it out.

Open Mic
Coffee Town
Music, poetry, and more
All are welcome!
Thursday, October 18, 6pm

I laughed out loud, immediately clasping my hand over my forehead in a pathetic attempt to block the pain. "That's tomorrow! Yeah. Like I'm going to do that."

"What are you talking about?" Marcus asked. "It's perfect! You get up there and you play your song and people besides me and Mom hear it."

"I don't know, man," I said.

Marcus's shoulders sagged a little. He looked frustrated with me. "C'mon, Sam. Seriously? You sit in that room every morning and every night and you play that song and it's awesome, man! You have to go public!"

"I can't. You don't get it. Everything is so easy for you."

Marcus inhaled sharply but said nothing. I was holding my head perfectly still to keep the ache at a minimum.

When Marcus finally spoke, exasperation sparked in his words. "You need to tell that voice in your head that says you can't do it to shove it. You *are* good enough. But you have to show up. Otherwise, what's the point? You just go through your life doing what people expect, no more, no less. You might as well be invisible. And I'm here to tell you that you should not be invisible. Your talent is…" he paused. "…It's undeniable. But if you don't put your stuff out there for people to see and hear, it doesn't matter. Talent only takes you to the door. *You* have to open it. You show up.

That's it! That's the secret, the money, the big mystery." He leaned toward me, his hands with straight fingers punctuating each word.

He stared at me for longer than was comfortable. I shifted in my seat.

"I'll think about it," I said. "I have to go lie down."

Marcus picked up the remote and leaned back on the couch. "I'm tellin' you, man…" His voice trailed off, like he had run out of gas. He let out a sigh that was audible as I walked to our shared room.

Sick

I was still asleep when Mom got home that night. She came in and put her hand on my forehead, then kissed my cheek. I tried to open my eyes, but it hurt too much.

"Did you take some aspirin, honey?" she asked. She stroked my hair, the same way she had done my whole life, every time I was sick. It made me want to curl up into a little ball on her lap. The smooth scent of her face cream wound its way into my nose.

"Mm-hmm."

"Do you want some dinner?"

"Unh-unh."

"Do you want me to leave you alone?"

No, I thought. *I want you to stay here all night and rub my back like when I was little.*

"Mm-hmm," I lied.

"Okay, I'll check on you in a bit." She rose from the edge of my bed and left the room. The door shut quietly.

I lay in bed listening to the murmurs of Mom and Marcus's voices rising and falling, not able to make out any of the words. I drifted off into a dream where I was on stage, playing the guitar. At first Dad was standing next to

68

me, then he was standing in the audience, and then I couldn't see him anymore.

And then
one day
your maybe-friend
is absent

Missiles launched
from turned heads and
diverted glances and
general disregard
whistle through the air
heat-seeking their target
screaming
"ALONE!"

Alone.

And you tighten
your laces
and your resolve
to keep your head
up.

Again.

Willa G. Vaughn

Remembering

Mom poked her head into our room the next morning. With one eye open I could see that she had her purse slung over her shoulder and an armload of files.

"Okay, kiddo, there's sandwich-makings in the fridge and not too much TV, got it? If you're staying home sick from school, you need to sleep."

"I know, Mom," I mumbled, my face half-buried in my pillow. She crossed the room to pet my hair, then gave me a kiss on the cheek. I grunted in reply and promptly fell back to sleep.

When I woke up again, it was well into the afternoon. My head felt like it was stuffed with cotton, but at least it wasn't pounding anymore. A loud rumble rose in my stomach as I rolled out of bed. I hadn't eaten in 24 hours.

A note was stuck to the fridge. *Not too much TV! Love you, Mom.* Ignoring the note, I took my plate to the couch and started to flip channels.

Mom hadn't set up streaming services in the apartment, so I was stuck with whatever was on during the day—in other words, a whole lot of nothing. After I cycled through all of the channels a couple of times I turned it off, set my empty plate in the sink, and went back to my room.

The flyer about the open mic was on the floor by my bed. Marcus must have put it there. I picked it up, then tossed it back down. No way I could get up and play my song in front of people. Only real musicians did that, and I was just a one-song kid whose dad taught him to pluck out some chords.

I pulled my guitar case out from under the bed and took the guitar out. Cradling it under my arm, I leaned over it and started to pick out the first few notes. Sometimes I played it more quickly, but today I felt like taking it slow. My thoughts drifted back to the day everything changed.

I was in my old room, sitting in my desk chair. Over the top of my guitar I could hear Mom and Dad's voices rising. I leaned over and pushed my door shut, then got back to the music.

Until a crash from the living room made me jump.

"What is WRONG with you?" I heard Mom yell. "Why do you keep doing this?"

"Nothing is WRONG with me!" Dad hollered. "Can't you see how hard I am trying?"

"You're NOT trying!" she screamed back. "You are drunk ALL of the time! Did you even go to that job interview today?"

Silence. I heard Mom's voice in a low mumble, but I couldn't make out her words. Then another crash. I jumped out of my chair, tossed the guitar on my bed, and opened the door at the same time that Marcus opened his. We locked eyes, and I followed him down the hall.

"My GOD!" she screamed. "You can't even stand up straight! I can't take this anymore!"

"Fine!" Dad yelled. "Don't even care!" His voice sounded like his words were all tied together with yarn. As Marcus turned into the living room, I could see Dad leaning on the back of the couch, swaying slightly. Two of our dining room chairs were lying on the floor.

"Dad…" Marcus said. I couldn't tell if it was a question or a warning.

Dad had been like this almost every day for the past few months. Most mornings he was still passed out when the rest of us left for the day, and when we got home we could always find him on the couch drinking beer and watching whatever sport was on TV Weekends were the worst. The three of us walked around him like he was roadkill.

"Shut up," Dad said to Marcus, looking vaguely in his direction. "This doesn't concern you." *Thisshdusntconshernnnyoo*.

"Don't tell him to shut up!" Mom couldn't contain her rage. She walked closer to Dad and got right in his face with her finger pointing angrily. "Don't you EVER talk like that to our boys!"

"Get your finger out of my face!" Dad swung his right arm up. His palm connected with Mom's cheek

Marcus and I froze as Mom wheeled away from Dad and fell to her hands and knees. She cradled the left side of her face with her hand, staring at the floor.

I couldn't breathe.

"Jenny…Jenny…I'm so sorry…are you…I didn't mean…" Dad fell to his knees behind her, swaying, steadying himself by grasping the back of the couch.

He reached out and touched Mom's back. She jerked away from him.

"Get away from me!" she wailed, still holding the side of her face. She looked over her shoulder at him as she rose to her feet. "Stay away!"

Mom stormed into their bedroom and slammed the door so hard the pictures on the wall swayed. Pictures of the four of us, individually and together, always smiling.

Dad looked stunned. Still on his knees, he buried his face in his hands. A sob escaped.

Marcus and I were frozen in place. Finally, after what felt like hours of standing there watching Dad weep and hearing Mom's muffled cries from the bedroom, Marcus pushed past me and went in his room, banging his door closed. After a moment, I followed, shutting my door with a soft click.

Throwing Punches

I snapped back into the present when I heard the front door slam. I realized that I had stopped playing my guitar; my hand was just dangling there next to the strings. I'd been so lost in the memory of the fight that I hadn't even noticed.

Just then the door opened and slammed again, this time so hard that the apartment shook. Who was home? And what was with the door slamming? I set my guitar down and rose to standing just as I heard Mom's voice.

"I can't *believe* this, Marcus!" she yelled. I froze, waiting. Maybe it would be better to hear what was going on from the safety of the bedroom. The light coming in the window was dim; it was later than I had realized.

"I *said* I was sorry," Marcus replied loudly, without a hint of apology in his voice.

"That's not good enough!" Mom shouted. "What were you *thinking*? What did that kid even do to you to deserve being punched?"

"I told you…"

"And *then* I find out you've been skipping classes? Are you *crazy*? You are going to get kicked out! And *then* what am I supposed to do?"

"I don't care!" Marcus hollered. "I don't care at all! I hate that stupid school! I hate this stupid apartment! I hate this town!" With each statement his voice grew louder and more furious. He wasn't done, either. "And I hate YOU for bringing us here!"

Then there was a loud crash. Then silence. I flung open the bedroom door and raced out into the living room.

The TV was lying on the rusty carpet, wires going every which way. Marcus's backpack was lying next to it, obviously the projectile that had knocked it off its base. Marcus was standing with his hands clenched by his sides, his chest rising and falling with quick, gasping breaths. Mom had her hands pressed to the sides of her head and was as still as stone.

"How dare you…?" Mom seethed.

"Mom, I'll pay for it," Marcus interrupted, a note of panic in his voice.

"I don't care about the TV," Mom said. She lowered her hands to her sides and glared daggers at Marcus. "How dare you blame *me* for this?"

Marcus was silent. Mom turned her fierce gaze at me, then directed it back at Marcus. "You boys think I want to be here? This isn't what I want! I *want* your dad to pull it together. I *want*…" Her eyes filled with tears, but she blinked and angrily wiped them away. "I asked *one* thing of both of you when we came here. *Try*. Try to be okay. Try your best at your new schools. That was all I wanted from you." A tear escaped and rolled down her cheek. "And you couldn't even do that."

Time trickled by as they stood there, defiantly staring at one another. Finally Marcus spoke.

"You're right, Mom. I couldn't do that. Just like I couldn't stop Dad from hitting you. I can't do anything right."

Her face fell. She reached out a hand as Marcus brushed past, but he didn't stop. "Marcus…" she said quietly.

He didn't meet my eyes as he pushed past me to go into our bedroom. The door slammed shut.

Mom looked at me with pleading eyes, but she didn't say anything. I had everything and nothing to say, all at once.

We stood like that for a long minute. Then she sighed loudly, wiped her face with both hands and went out the front door.

Nowhere to Go

Their words bounced through my head as I stood in the living room, staring at the bare beige walls. Marcus was skipping classes? And he *punched* someone? Mom thought we weren't *trying*? I felt a knot forming in my throat. All we had done was try. Try to stay out of Dad's way. Try to survive at new schools where we didn't know anyone.

I attempted to pick up the TV, but it was too awkward to lift by myself. I walked slowly back through the hallway, my bare toes sinking into the graying carpet, and gently opened the door to our shared bedroom. Marcus was stretched out on his bed, his feet a centimeter away from hanging off the edge. He was still wearing his coat and shoes. Headphones were clapped over his ears and his eyes were glued to the ceiling. His jaw was working overtime. Avoiding having my head ripped off seemed like the smart choice, so I backed out of the room as quietly as I had entered.

With nothing to do and a desperate need to get away from the apartment, I remembered the open mic. I grabbed my shoes and jacket from the entryway where I'd dropped them the day before, and I headed out the door.

"Hey Gus," I said as I stepped out onto the front step. "Did you see my mom go by a while ago?"

"Hey, man, I sure did," Gus said. He looked at me and I noticed for the first time that his eyes were a little cloudy. "She looked down in the dumps. Y'all doin' okay over there?"

"Uh, yeah," I faltered. "Um, she just, uh, she and my brother had an argument."

"Yeah, man, I heard the yelling," Gus said. He tapped his head with his forefinger. "I know how that goes. My boy and I used to go at it, too, fightin' like roosters."

"Did you see where she went?"

"She went down toward the waterfront," Gus said, flipping his wrist in that direction. "Asked me to keep an eye out for the two of you while she walked a bit."

I took a breath and sighed. "Thanks, Gus. If she comes back, will you tell her I'll be back soon? And that I left a note on the counter?"

"Yeah, man, I'll do that."

I shoved my hands in my jeans pockets as I walked away from the apartment, past the fountain. Brown leaves crunched under my feet as I moved down the brick path to the sidewalk and turned left. It was already starting to get dark, and I shivered, squeezing my sides to keep the brisk air from piercing my skin.

Open Mic

The coffee shop was nestled in the strip mall between a frozen yogurt shop and a hair salon. I cut through the parking lot and walked toward it. As I pulled the door open, I heard a smattering of applause and cheers.

"Hi!" A perky voice at my elbow caught my attention as I walked in. I glanced down to see a woman sitting at a table with a pad of paper in front of her. "You want to put your name on the list?"

I must have given her a dopey blank look because she smiled and tapped the pad with her black fingernail. "The list. To perform?" she said. She had a tattoo of a vine winding around her forearm, starting at her wrist and disappearing into her pushed up sleeve.

"Um, no, thanks," I mumbled. "I'm just watching."

She looked at me steadily through thick eye makeup, then sucked air through her teeth. "Well, next time then, yeah?" she said. Did she know something about me?

I shrugged and walked up to the closest empty seat, a stool alongside the wall.

"All right, next up, we have a poem by…"

A large man stood behind the microphone in an open corner by the counter. He had wild curly hair and those circular earrings that make the hole in the earlobe huge. He wore a shirt with a drawing of a bone and the words *I found this humerus*. It took me a minute to get the joke, and in the meantime I missed the poet's name.

The poet cleared his throat directly into the microphone and began reading. His poem was about sunlight and trees and a girlfriend who left him. As he read, I studied him. He was not that old, actually—maybe like 25 or 30. He wore a button-down shirt with Western designs and rumpled jeans. His voice held so much expression that it was almost as if he was performing it rather than reading. It went loud, then soft, then filled with humor that made the audience chuckle, then turned sad. I heard heartbreak and loss in his words, but also forgiveness and love. I was captivated, and disappointed when it was over.

As the audience applauded, I glanced around the room and made eye contact with Willa.

Wait, what?

Willa was looking right at me from across the room with an expression I couldn't quite read. Her long hair was pulled over one shoulder. She sat next to a man who looked—from what I could tell by the back of his head—as if he was talking to her. Then he turned around to follow her gaze and next thing I knew I was looking at Willa's eyes in a man's face.

"Okay, folks, let's keep it going for a song by Hannah!" The host clapped as he stepped back behind from the microphone, and a girl who looked to be in high school with a guitar around her neck moved toward it. As she began to strum a familiar pop song, I looked back toward Willa. She was clearly talking to the man, which was a sight I had never seen. The man once again turned to look at me, this time with a grin. Willa kept her eyes on the performer, and she and the man both clapped as she finished.

I felt a sudden urge to leave. What was I doing there? I slid forward on my stool, looking down to make sure I didn't step on anything.

"Hi, Sam, is it?"

The man's voice surprised me and I was caught in an awkward half-on, half-off position on the stool. I looked up and again saw Willa's eyes in his face.

He chuckled a little. "Sorry, didn't mean to startle you. I'm Willa's dad. Do you want to come join us?"

"Oh, um, I was gonna go…" I stuttered.

"No, c'mon, come sit with us," he said. "There is an empty seat at our table." He hovered over me, much taller and more solid than my own dad. He clapped a hand on my shoulder and guided me toward Willa as the host came back behind the mic to announce the next act.

Willa looked at me as I sat down. "Hi," I said. She grinned and rolled her eyes. It was an *oh my god my dad is so embarrassing* look.

As a harmonica player took his place behind the microphone, Willa's dad leaned across the table. "Willa tells me you have a class together," he whispered.

"Yeah, language arts," I answered.

"Ah, the favorite class!" he said a little louder, lightly punching Willa's shoulder. She rolled her eyes again and shook her head. Her pink and purple fingertips pulled at the ends of her hair.

The harmonica player was not very good, and I was glad when he was done. Willa's dad leaned across the table again. "I keep bringing

Willa to these open mics. I want her to read one of her poems up there."

"Dad!" she blurted. Her voice came out of nowhere. "Stop!"

"Sorry, sorry. She doesn't like it when I tell people she's a poet." Her dad leaned back against his chair, but then leaned forward again conspiratorially. "She's really good." He laughed as she punched him—hard—in the shoulder. "Sorry, sorry. I won't do it again."

I looked back at Willa. Despite her warning, despite the hard punch, she had a big smile and her cheeks were flushed.

Her voice had sounded so...*normal*.

Two singers, one monologue and a bongo player later, the host thanked us all for coming and reminded us that the open mic ran on the same night every month. "See y'all in November!" he crowed as people began to rise from their seats.

"Hey, Sam," Willa's dad said as we made our way toward the door. "We always go next door for frozen yogurt after this. Want to join us?"

"Um..." I looked at Willa. Her eyes were bright, and she raised her eyebrows expectantly. "Um, I didn't bring any money."

"Our treat!" Willa's dad's hand clapped my shoulder again, and we stepped out into the dark evening.

Just an Ordinary Conversation

The frozen yogurt shop's fluorescent light blinded me as I stepped in behind Willa and her dad. As my eyes adjusted, bright blue chairs against white plastic tables came into focus. Two women and a little boy sat at a corner table. Along the wall, at least 15 spouts were labeled with flavors like Cheesecake Dream, Mooka Mocha and Very Vanilla. A stainless steel bar displayed a massive variety of candies, fruits and other toppings. I served myself a small cup of Strawberry Sunrise and piled it with gummy bears and M&Ms.

We settled at a table by the window. Since it was dark out, I could see my reflection as clearly as if I was looking in a mirror. Willa sat across from me, and her dad settled in next to her.

"So, Sam, Willa tells me you're new to Brooks," Willa's dad said, licking his spoon. "What do you think so far?"

I paused, swallowing my bite. "It's fine, I guess. For a school."

"Are you finding new friends okay?" This question caught me off guard. It seemed kind of personal for someone who didn't know me.

"I guess," I replied. "I kind of miss my old school."

Willa's dad glanced at Willa, then leaned his head toward her. "You look like you want to say something," he murmured. "What is it?"

There was a long pause, during which her lips opened and closed several times. She looked at her yogurt.

"Why…" Her voice was soft. "Why did you move?"

It was the first thing she'd ever said to me. And it was a question I really, really didn't want to answer.

"Um, my parents, uh, my mom…" I stammered, then stopped.

"Hey, Sam, it's all right to keep it to yourself." Willa's dad broke the silence. He gave me a gentle smile, so kind that it made me look down and stir my yogurt. Gummy bears and M&Ms were sinking as it melted. "But Willa's a good listener if you ever want to talk."

I heard the bell on the door jingle, and I looked over my shoulder. An older woman walked in with a huge smile on her face, followed closely by Mr. Wheadon, my math teacher. He looked as much a mess as usual, with his wrinkled coat and gray hair sticking every which direction. But he also had a big grin on his face—something I'd never seen— and they leaned their heads together as though they were sharing a secret as they walked up to the yogurt dispensers.

"Good old Mr. Wheadon," Willa's dad said quietly. "He was teaching back when I went to Brooks, can you believe it? He was everyone's favorite teacher."

"*Seriously?*" I couldn't help myself.

"Yeah," he said. "But then his wife died. I heard he kind of shut down, started just going through the motions." Willa's dad paused, then chuckled quietly. "Looks like he's doing all right now, though!"

I kept stirring. The subject was super awkward, so I forced myself to change it.

"So that notebook you have? At school?" I asked, glancing up at Willa. "Is that for your poems?" She nodded. It looked like words were sitting right on the tip of her tongue, but none came out.

"Willa has been writing poems since she could hold a pencil," her dad said proudly. "Every once in a while, she lets her mom and I read them. But that's only when we beg."

Willa grinned, and her cheeks flushed.

"I think it's hard to share your art, some-times," her dad continued. "But I'll tell you this: if I had any talent I would be out on the street corner making everyone who strolled by watch and listen." We all laughed.

Willa spoke again. "You make good pan-cakes." Her voice made me think of a small rabbit skittering from one hiding place to an-other. Her dad seemed unfazed, as though he heard her voice all the time.

"Ah, yes, the Great Pancake Maker," her dad chuckled. "I should really take that show on the road." We laughed again and finished our yogurts.

"Do you have a talent we should know about?" I realized he was asking me.

"Well, I play the guitar, a little," I an-swered. "My brother thinks I should play at that open mic."

"Hey, now, if you do that you be sure to let us know!" Willa's dad voice bounded around the room. "That's outstanding!"

"Uh, yeah, okay." I blushed. I suddenly re-alized that I had been gone for a long time. "Thank you for the yogurt," I said, pushing my chair back. "I think I need to get home."

"You are most welcome. It was my pleas-ure to meet you." Willa's dad stuck out his hand, like we were business colleagues or something. His large fingers wrapped around mine and he shook my hand firmly. "Hope to see you again sometime."

"Yeah," I said. I looked at Willa. "Bye."

"Bye," she answered softly. Her eyes flickered up to me, and her face seemed to say *wait, one more thing*. But she looked back down at her yogurt.

As the bell on the door jingled behind me, I felt like the breath I'd been holding since I'd moved here had finally been exhaled.

Everything's Okay...

When I got home, Marcus and Mom were sitting on the couch, close enough that they were almost touching. Their faces were drawn. Marcus had dark circles under his eyes and Mom's cheeks were covered in fading red splotches. A cop show flickered on the TV—apparently no harm was done by the angry flying backpack.

"Hi, kiddo," Mom said tiredly. "What were you doing at the coffee shop?"

I kicked off my shoes and shrugged my coat onto the chair next to the door. "There was an open mic. I just went to watch."

Marcus locked eyes with me but didn't say anything. He looked too tired to tease me about going, even after his prodding the day before.

"How's your headache?" Mom asked.

"Better."

"Come sit." She patted the couch on the other side of her. I walked around behind them and flopped beside her.

"TV works, huh?" I said.

"Yep. It's okay. Everything's okay." She put a hand on each of our thighs. "I love you guys."

We sat like that for the rest of the evening, everything said and not said swirling around us as though we were in the eye of a hurricane.

Weird but true, I think I have a new friend. Don't freak out, but he's a boy

You have a boy-friend? HAHAHAHAHAHAHAHA

Sorry, couldn't help it

I'm glad you have someone to talk to.

U mad?

Sorry Jack was in my room. Annoying!!

So, who's this dude, anyway?

Sam. He's in my Language Arts class with me. Was at the open mic last night. Dad dragged him to fro-yo like we used to. Seems nice.

Cool! Did you read a poem?

No. Too scared.

Someday you won't be.

NOVEMBER

Partners

"Are you sure this will work?" I whispered to Willa.

Willa nodded. She was already scribbling away in her notebook.

"I don't know. Maybe we should have asked first." I slumped back in my seat.

She poked me in the arm with the cap of her pen. I looked at her, and her expression made me laugh. *Trust me, dummy.*

"Good morning everyone!" Ms. Abaroa chirped. Her hair was in braids, and the ropes bounced as she walked across the room. "Ready for presentations today?"

There were some groans. "Now, relax, people. It isn't about right and wrong, just your best thinking. This is your chance to teach each other what you found when you dug into some poems. Alright, let's see. I think Jose and Max are going first, right guys?"

I felt a little bad for Max, because Jose had volunteered them to go first. At least I knew Willa wouldn't do that.

The day after the open mic, Ms. Abaroa told me that partners for this project had been selected while I was home sick. Willa was left without a partner at the end of class, and so Ms. Abaroa paired us up. I was surprised—and also not surprised—that Willa hadn't said anything when I had seen her the night before.

She and I ignored the assignment for a week or so. Then, a couple of days before it was due, Willa passed me a note inviting me to her house so that we could work on it.

When I rang the doorbell at her house, I instantly heard footsteps running toward the door and a voice yelling, "I'll get it!" The door swung open. The kid's lower legs were thick with soccer shin guards and he held a plastic sword. His eyes widened as he looked up at me.

"Is Willa here?" I asked.

"Hi, you must be Sam! I'm Jack. Willa's in her room. WILLA! WILL-A! WILLAAAAA! Oh, you can come in. My mom's not here, she's at work, but my dad's here. He works from home. DAD! WILLA'S FRIEND IS HERE. Hey, do you play soccer?" Listening to Jack, I understood how someone could literally talk a mile a minute. I shook my head, but he didn't wait for my response. "I was just going to get a snack and watch a show. Do you watch Pokémon? It's awesome." Jack scampered off and left me standing in the entryway of their house.

The late-afternoon sun streamed in through a window above the door and dust particles floated in its wake. Willa's dad stuck his head from around a corner.

"Hi, Sam! C'mon in. Willa will be right down."

I followed him down a short hallway into the kitchen. Bright yellow walls and white cabinets gave the room a cheery feel.

"How've you been?" Willa's dad asked. "You still playing that guitar?"

"Yeah," I replied, flattered that he remembered. I spotted Willa's backpack hanging on the back of a wooden chair, one of four circling the round kitchen table.

Willa's dad followed my gaze. "Willa said you'd be working there at the table. I'll get out of your hair." He set some crackers next to sliced cheese on a plate and brushed crumbs from his hands. "Jack! Here's your snack!" he hollered. "You want anything, Sam?"

"No, thank you," I said.

"Okay, well, make yourself comfortable. I'm sure Willa will be right down. JACK! Ugh," said Willa's dad. "I guess I will serve His Highness." With a grin he took a deep bow, picked up the plate, and left the kitchen.

As I settled into a chair, something brushed against my leg. Startled, I looked down. A gray and brown tabby cat was circling next to my foot, rubbing against my jeans with each pass. It wore a bright blue collar with tags that jingled. I stuck my hand down to pet it, but it jumped back and stared at me.

"Here kitty, kitty," I quietly sang. "Come here, kitty kitty."

"She won't." Willa's quiet voice surprised me.

"Oh, hey," I said, looking up. "Why not?"

Willa shrugged and sat down in the chair beside me, placing a folded laptop on the table. "She's a chicken," she murmured. "Aren't you, Sapphire?" She stuck her hand down alongside her leg and the cat rubbed up against it once before scampering away.

"She was a stray," Willa said. "We got her a year ago. Someone found her and her brother in that empty lot by school." She was looking at her lap as the words tumbled out of her.

Then she looked at me and blinked expectantly.

"Huh," I said, at a loss. It was the most I'd ever heard her say. I decided to change the subject. "So, what should we do first?"

She shrugged, then reached over and with a bright purple nail tapped the binder I'd brought along.

"Oh, right, the poem," I said, answering her unasked question. "Yeah, I have it." I dug in my binder and pulled out the poem Ms. Abaroa had assigned us. I smoothed it out before handing it to Willa. "I haven't read it yet."

She looked at me with one eyebrow up. She thrust it back at me, but I put my hand up. "Why don't you just read it aloud? That way we both hear it," I suggested.

Her eyelids lowered slightly, and her shoulders dropped. She didn't want to read it aloud, I could tell. She blinked a bunch of times in a row.

Uh-oh. Was she going to cry?

I didn't understand why words came easily to her one minute and not the next. I wanted to snatch it back from her, to take the pressure off her. Mostly, I didn't want to make her cry.

The problem was, and had always been, that I couldn't count on my brain to put the letters in the right order. Mostly, I didn't want to show my stupidity in front of Willa.

Ugh.

"*Fine*," I said. "Hand it over." I stared at the page until the letters settled down. Finally, they all landed in orderly rows. But were they in the right order? I wasn't so sure. I took a deep breath and began.

We never know how high we are
by Emily Dickenson

We never know how high we are
Till we are called to rise;
And then, if we are true to plan,
Our statures touch the skies—

The Heroism we recite
Would be a daily thing,
Did not ourselves the Cubits warp
For fear to be a King—

Fortunately, the poem was short. Unfortunately, I had no clue what any of it meant. When I looked up, relieved that I had only stumbled on a couple of words, Willa was staring at me with an unreadable expression.

"What?" I asked.

She shrugged, reaching for the poem. I snatched it away from her.

"*What?*" I snarled. I was on the defensive. Did I read it wrong? Of course I did.

She sat back in her seat and took a deep breath, exhaling loudly. The cat was circling around her feet, letting out the occasional *mew*.

"It..." she began. She inhaled again and blew the air through her pursed lips toward the ceiling. "It..."

In the split second between feeling edgy about my reading skills and thinking about running out the door, I noticed that Willa was really trying to get words out. Her cheeks and lips were flexing and clenching, as if they were trying to squeeze her words out like a toothpaste tube.

One deep breath later: "It was a cool poem."

I looked at her with confusion. "Wait, that made sense to you?"

She nodded.

"I didn't understand it at all," I said. "I'm not even sure I said it right. It's like Greek or something."

Willa made a weird sound, a combination of a giggle and a snort, and shook her head. Her eyes were filled with laughter.

I looked back at the words, but the letters were floating around the page again. I sighed and shook my head. "I really hate poetry," I muttered under my breath.

"Why?" The word flew from her throat and soared across the table. Each word seemed like a gift, offered when you least expected it.

I shrugged, still looking at the paper.

She pushed her next words out in a breathy rush. "Reading is hard for you."

It wasn't a question, and I didn't offer a response.

"Okay," she said. She snatched the poem from me and tapped her forehead with a grin. *I know what to do.*

Presenting...

"As Jose and Max get ready, I'll just quickly review the expectations. You are going to read your assigned poem to the class, and then give us a brief analysis, including explicit and implied meanings and your reactions to it." Ms. Abaroa walked up and down the aisles between desks, patting a shoulder here and there as kids began to settle down. "Alright, boys, you're up!"

Jose and Max looked about as thrilled as gorillas in captivity as they trudged up to the front of the class. Jose read the poem, then Max read directly from a half-sheet of scribbled notes. They were done in one minute flat, and the class gave them a paltry round of applause.

"Okay, who's next? Oh, Sam and Willa, great!" I whirled around to look at Willa. She was looking at her desk, but sure enough her arm was floating in the air as if it had gone up of its own will. She drew it down and looked at me sheepishly.

I scowled at her. I rose from my seat and fished in my front pocket for the flash drive

Willa's dad had given us. "So, um, we did a Powerpoint."

Ms. Abaroa waved me up to the computer at the front of the room. "Super! I love visual presentations. You can stand off to the side while you talk so that the class can see the screen."

My stomach twisted. I knew this was a bad idea. We should have asked first.

"Actually," I blurted. "We don't need to talk. It's all on the Powerpoint."

Ms. Abaroa blinked at me. She looked at Willa, still sitting in the back of the room with her head down, and back at me. She scratched her head with one fingernail between her thin braids. Then she nodded slightly. "So, volume up, then?" she asked.

"Yes, please." I handed her the flash drive and returned to my seat.

"Okay. Let's see what we've got. Keith, will you get the lights?"

As the lights went out, Emily Dickinson's poem came up on the screen. Jack's voice blasted from the speakers, and Ms. Abaroa scrambled to turn the volume down. Laughter bubbled around the room.

"Alright, alright," she said. "Settle down. Let's try that again."

Jack's voice entered the room again, his enthusiasm rivaled only by his strain to not talk about other things. I was skeptical about a kid his age reading the poem aloud, but Willa had quietly assured me he could do it. We'd had to record him reading it several times because he kept interjecting his own thoughts.

"What's a cubit?" Click. Start over.

"Hey, my friend Diego is super tall." Click.

"What's this poem about, anyway? She writes weird." CLICK.

As Jack finished the second stanza, our thought bubbles popped up. Putting our analysis of the poem into thought bubbles was Willa's idea, and it turned out pretty good. It was my idea to define "Cubits"—we had to Google it and we figured no one else would know what it meant either.

We all have greatness inside of us.

Our fear is what keeps us from being truly great.

We measure ourselves incorrectly, and think we have to be something other than what we are.

A Cubit was a unit of measurement in Emily Dickenson's time.

As the last bubble popped up, Ms. Abaroa gestured to Keith to turn the lights back on. "Very creative presentation," she said, looking at Willa and I with an expression that was hard to read. "I guess I never said you had to talk."

Grumbles rippled across the classroom. "Seriously?" somebody muttered. The truth is the presentation had probably taken us way longer than it had taken anyone else to prepare. But when kids hear about a loophole they didn't think of, they feel cheated.

Willa poked me in the arm with the eraser end of her pencil. *See?* she said without saying anything. *All good.*

Missed Opportunities

When the bell rang at the end of class, Ms. Abaroa asked Willa and me to stay back. As the rest of the class jostled and shoved their way out of the room, we stood shoulder to shoulder in front of her desk.

Ms. Abaroa put her elbows on her desk and folded her hands under her chin. "You two worked around the system today. You were supposed to give an oral presentation." Neither of us responded.

Ms. Abaroa sighed and stood up. "Listen, your analysis of the poem was good, and your presentation was creative. But it wasn't what I asked you to do. If you have trouble speaking"—with this she gestured toward Willa—"or reading"—here she pointed her gaze at me—"I am happy to help you figure out alternatives. But I need you to keep me in the loop, okay? We're a team here." She came around the desk and sat on the edge, right in front of us. "I know that both of you have things that make school difficult. But I'm on your side. Don't forget that."

Students in her next class began to trickle in. "You two better get going," she said. We both turned toward the door. "Hey, Sam?" Ms.

Abaroa said. I looked back at her. "Will you please come back during lunch, when you're finished eating? I'd like to have a quick word."

I nodded and followed Willa out the classroom door. Ms. Abaroa's words bounced around in my head. Trouble reading? I thought I had hidden it pretty well. Why did she want to talk to me? Please, I begged the universe. Don't let it be a special reading class.

I trailed behind Willa, lost in thought, until Willa almost ran smack into Ashley. Ashley was waiting outside the door like a vulture who had spotted prey.

"What, you had to have your baby brother read the poem because you were too scared?" Though her expression looked innocent enough, an ugly sneer laced Ashley's words. Willa stepped to the right, trying to move past Ashley and the two girls behind her. "Couldn't your *boyfriend* do it?" I froze. This was not good.

Willa's shoulders tensed up as she tried again to step around Ashley, who leaned in menacingly. "Oh, did you want to say something?" scoffed Ashley.

I knew I should step in. I knew I should say something. I knew.

But I turned and walked away.

I walk on
your words,
the hot coals burn my feet.

(I am fireproof;
silent air in my lungs
my shield.)

I swim through
your words,
the maelstrom slams my limbs.

(I can float
on the surface
at peace.)

Willa G. Vaughn

Regret

I felt horrible for the rest of the morning. I hid in the bathroom during lunch until it was time to go to see Ms. Abaroa.

I tried to justify walking away from Willa and Ashley, the way I didn't stand up for us. I told myself that I didn't want to add fuel to what Ashley was saying about my being Willa's boyfriend. That's not what we were.

But were we friends?

I thought we were, but it's not like we had spent any time together except for that poetry assignment.

It was easy, hanging out with her.

But she didn't talk, and don't you have to talk if you want to be a friend?

My mind spun as I walked toward the Language Arts classroom. The only thing I knew for sure was that, whether we were friends or not, I should have said something.

Ms. Abaroa sat at her desk, eating a sandwich. She saw me standing in the doorway and waved me in, wiping her mouth with the back of her hand and closing the book she was reading. She had a mouthful of food, and as she chewed she pointed me over to a desk, walked over and sat down next to me.

I waited anxiously until she finally swallowed. "Sorry," she grinned. "I always end up shoving food in my face as quick as I can. Not a lot of time to eat around here." She cleared her throat and wiped the corners of her mouth with her fingertips. Leaning toward me, she tilted her head slightly.

"Sam," she said. "Reading is challenging for you, isn't it?"

I groaned inwardly. I knew it. I didn't say anything.

"Okay, listen," Ms. Abaroa said. Her voice was kind. "I get it. Have you ever had any reading support? Special classes or extra practice with an adult in school?"

Back in elementary school, I'd been part of a small reading group that left the classroom every day. But it didn't really seem to help and all it did was make it so that when I got back to class I didn't know what was going on. Then at Lyndale Middle, in sixth grade, no one seemed to notice.

I didn't tell Ms. Abaroa any of this. I just nodded.

"Sam, I know it's hard to feel different. Trust me, I know." She gave me a look that made me think that maybe she *did* know. But

I was afraid of where this was going. I remained quiet.

She looked at me steadily for what felt like forever. Then she said the words all teachers say. "Reading is really important, Sam."

"I know," I muttered.

"What we need to do is help you develop some strategies that will make it easier for you. You don't need to do more than everyone else. You just need to do it more intentionally and in specific ways. Think of a dog with three legs."

"What?"

She laughed. "A dog with three legs can walk, but he has to do it differently than dogs with four. That's what we need to figure out for you. Your different mode of walking...er, reading." She smiled. "I'm going to help you find it."

I shook my head. I really had no idea what she was talking about.

"Before we do that, Sam, I'm going to ask the reading teacher here to do a few assessments with you. Just to see where your strengths are and what specific parts of reading you struggle with. Is that okay?"

I shrugged. It sounded like torture.

"Good. I will talk to her after school and maybe she can squeeze you in later this week or early next week." Ms. Abaroa stood, so I did too. She put her hand on my shoulder, and I realized for the first time that I was the same height as her. "It's going to be fine, Sam. We are going to figure this out. Just don't pretend with me, okay?"

I nodded again and left the classroom.

Second Chances

Life at the apartment had gotten a little better after Mom and Marcus's big fight. Mom had gone out of her way to do things with us, including having what she called "chat time" after dinner. It was supposed to be our time to talk about what had happened with Dad, to ask our questions, and to get honest answers. Usually neither Marcus nor I had any questions, because we knew that her answer was going to be "I don't know" or "When your dad gets his act together." But Marcus promised that he wouldn't skip any more classes, and Mom called the school daily to make sure.

One afternoon, while we'd watched college basketball after school, Marcus told me that he had been going to the skate park when he ditched his classes. I was confused, because he didn't own a skateboard and as far as I knew he'd never skated. But Marcus said that during the day there was usually only this one guy there, and that watching him skate was like watching LeBron play basketball.

"Huh," I said.

"It all just gets to be too much," he continued. "Dad being a drunk and Mom moving us here, and then having to be around all of these new people..." He trailed off and then abruptly changed the subject. "I know alcoholism's a disease or whatever, but I used to think that they'd do anything for us, you know? I'm so mad at him. Mom too. Like, *all* of the time."

I looked at him out of the corner of my eye. He was chewing on his bottom lip.

"You don't seem mad all of the time. Sometimes yeah, but mostly you seem, like, easy-going and cool with everything." I didn't need to mention his recent outburst. It hung over the three of us like a fog.

"Yeah, well," He scratched his cheek and sighed. "I'm not."

"Why'd you punch that guy anyway?"

Marcus shrugged. "He got in my face."

"About what?"

"Okay, so, I was in line for a burger in the cafeteria, right? And this loser comes up to the girl in front of me, right? And he starts trying to put his arm around her and says all this stuff, and she was all like, 'Stop it' and trying to get away from him but I think she didn't want to lose her place in line, and then I said

'Hey man, she said stop' and then he got up in my face and said some stuff and I punched him." His words flew out of him in a *whoosh* of air, and then he paused.

"Whoa," I exhaled. "Overreact much?

He nodded. "Like I said, I'm mad all the time." Then, with no warning, he smashed a couch pillow into my face. "So you'd better watch out, you little punk."

"Oh, yeah?" I hollered, standing up with the pillow locked and loaded above my head.

We beat each other with pillows until Mom got home from work and told us to knock it off. Marcus grinned wickedly and threw a pillow at her.

Laughing like that, the three of us together, felt like cool cream on a sunburn.

Reparations

I dragged my feet as I walked home from school. Between Ms. Abaroa, Ashley, and my failure to stand up for Willa, I felt like a piece of garbage.

As I passed the strip mall where the coffee shop sat, I spotted a familiar purple backpack strapped to a back on the other side of the parking lot.

"Willa!" I shouted.

She turned away from the poster she was reading and looked around expectantly. When she saw me, she scowled and turned back around.

The need to fix my mistake overwhelmed me. Scurrying across the parking lot, I shouted her name again. She didn't turn around, but she didn't walk away, either.

"Hey," I panted as I arrived in front of the coffee shop window. "What're you doing?"

She didn't turn to look at me but pointed to the poster. It was an advertisement for a local all-ages poetry competition. I glanced at the side of her face, but her expression was unreadable. She turned and started to walk away.

"Hey," I said again. "Hey, Willa."

She stopped and turned toward me, keeping her eyes on her purple shoes. Her hair hung like walls on either side of her face.

"I, uh, I'm sorry I didn't help you with Ashley today," I muttered uncomfortably.

She dug the toe of one of her high-tops into the cement like she was trying to bore a hole.

"What's her deal, anyway? Why does she talk to you like that?" I asked.

Willa shrugged and pulled her backpack up higher on her shoulders. She tucked one wall of hair behind an ear.

"Well, she sucks," I said. "She sucks, like, a lot."

Willa glanced up at me, her eyes squinted and her eyebrows knitted together. A small smirk curled one side of her mouth.

"Yeah," I said, feeling a surge of confidence. "She sucks eggs."

A giggle escaped Willa's lips. Her hand flew from her backpack strap to cover her mouth as her eyes formed a question. *What?*

"I don't know," I said. "I heard that in this old movie my mom made us watch with her." It was a stupid insult, and I suddenly had a picture in my mind of Ashley sucking on an egg, her mouth puckered around it and her cheeks pulling in like a fish. I started laughing, and Willa did, too.

"I am really sorry," I repeated as I gasped for air. "I should have said something."

Willa shrugged again, but this time her eyes were bright and her face seemed relaxed. We said our goodbyes—well, I did, and she smiled—and then we both turned and walked away.

I promised myself that I wouldn't disappoint her again.

Fear
Of
Rejection
Gives anger an
Icy
Veneer.
Empty
Nothingness
Ending when
Someone
Smiles.

Willa G. Vaughn

Things are looking up

I could tell as soon as I walked into math class that something was different. It took me a minute to realize that Mr. Wheadon was standing in front of his desk, rather than sitting behind it. As students walked in, he greeted each of us by name and even shook a few hands, as if meeting us for the first time. Maybe in a way he was.

Once we were all seated, he stood in front of us like Superman, legs apart, chest puffed out, and hands on his hips.

"All right then," he said. "Who'd like to do some math?"

We all looked around at each other. Isn't that what we always do in this class?

"I don't mean your homework responses," he said. Apparently, mind-reading was one of his new superpowers. "I mean some real math. Some *exciting* math. Some math to really get your juices flowing."

A few giggles floated around the room, but still no one said anything. I think we were all in shock.

"I'm in the mood for some good problem solving," he crowed. Picking up the remote, he turned on the projector and a lengthy word problem appeared. The letters jumbled about as usual, but I could pick out that it was about video gamers and average scores.

"Let the problem solving begin!" he shouted and did a little dance. We all burst out laughing.

Where Do You Go?

"Alright, poets," Ms. Abaroa proclaimed a few days later. "Now that you are experts in analyzing poetry, you are going to write some of your own. Remember, we've studied both poems in specific structures and poems in free verse. What you write is entirely up to you, but your final portfolio will include..." Ms. Abaroa began to pass out papers which contained the assignment.

I glanced over at Willa. For the first time that I'd seen, she was looking right at Ms. Abaroa as our teacher described the assignment. Her eyes were bright. Figures, I thought, since poetry is her thing. I looked at the list of expected criteria in front of me and sighed. The words were dancing all over the page.

"And, big news!" Ms. Abaroa proclaimed. "There is a community-wide poetry competition happening, and you will each be submitting one of your poems! It culminates in an evening celebration at the high school next month, where the winners read their poems and ..."

"Will there be food?" asked Max. Everyone snickered.

"Yes, Max, there will be cake and coffee and tea, that sort of thing."

"Ooh, tea," said Ashley, rolling her eyes. *"Fancy."* The class laughed again.

"Okay, it's not a feast, but it is a really cool opportunity for writers to come together," said Ms. Abaroa, shaking her head slightly. She had lost some of her previous enthusiasm, and now looked like a half-deflated balloon. "Listen, if you attend the event, I will count it as extra credit. Now please take out your writing notebooks."

As students began to shuffle through their belongings, I slouched down in my seat. As much as I hated reading, writing was a close second. I felt a tap on my ankle and saw Willa's purple sneaker whip back under her desk like an animal in a burrow. I looked up at her. *You okay?* her expression read.

I shook my head. "This is going to suck." She giggled, then said in a voice I almost didn't hear: "Suck eggs."

I laughed. Just then, Ms. Abaroa arrived next to my desk. "Sam, can I have a quick word?" I looked up at her, and she leaned down to talk into my ear. "I left a message for your mom today, asking if she could come in and talk with you and I about the results of the reading assessment, and a plan for moving forward. I just didn't want you to be surprised when she brings it up." She stood back up and moved down the aisle. "Notebooks out, people!" she said again. "Let's not waste our precious time!"

I sighed. This wasn't going to go away. I had spent two hours with the reading teacher the day before, doing every sort of reading and writing task a person could think of.

Willa tossed a note onto my desk.

I can help you with your poems if you want.

"Really?" I whispered as the class began to settle into writing. "Can you write them for me?"

Her face contorted. *Fine, if you don't want help...*

"No, I'm kidding," I whispered. "Yes, please help. Do you want to come over after school today?"

She reached for the note she'd handed me and scribbled a few more words on it.

I'll check with my dad during lunch.

Then she bent over her notebook and began writing.

I looked at mine, open to a blank page. Sighing, I slid lower in my chair. This was definitely going to suck eggs.

Later that afternoon, Willa and I sat at the table in the apartment. Marcus wasn't home yet, and Mom had told us she'd be late and would bring home burgers for dinner. I was again slouched in my chair, staring at an empty page.

Willa occupied herself by looking around the apartment, taking in the beige walls, old furniture, and general blandness of the space. I could see her mouth opening and closing, like she was working on getting some words out.

"When…" she finally managed.

"We moved here in September," I said. "It was kind of sudden." She nodded and continued to look around.

"Where…" she tried again, and hesitated.

"We moved from Lyndale," I replied.

She shook her head. "Where is…" She paused again, then shook her head and looked at her hands, folded in her lap.

"It's okay," I said. "I'll just tell you stuff, and you can try again if I don't answer your question, okay?"

She looked at me, relief melting her crinkled brow.

"I live here with my mom and my brother," I began. "My brother's in high school. I didn't think we were going to stay here that long, but..." I stopped, unsure how to continue. "We, um, we left my dad. It's complicated."

She nodded, then reached over and patted my hand with her black and yellow fingertips. I realized I'd been drilling a hole in the paper of my notebook with the tip of my pencil. She took the pencil out of my hand and tapped it on my notebook.

"Poetry?" she asked quietly. She was changing the subject and I was relieved. I nodded.

She wrote something in her notebook and turned it so that I could read it.

What do you care about?

I looked at her quizzically. "What do you mean?"

She scribbled in her book again, and again turned it so that I could read it.

That's what you write about.

"Oh, right," I mumbled, and shrugged. "I dunno, my family, I guess. Music." She scribbled and turned her book.

Guitar?

"Yeah."

Scribble. Turn.

Why guitar?

"I guess because I can relax, or escape, or something."

Where do you go?

"What?"

She rolled her eyes.

When you escape?

"I dunno."

She sat back in her chair and looked at me. I couldn't read her expression; it almost looked like she was trying to read my mind. Then she grinned, wrote something, and pushed the notebook toward me.

Play right now.

"No way."

She tapped her note and nodded.

"NO WAY," I said again, shaking my head.

She shrugged and, once again, her face said *Fine, if you don't want help…*

I groaned and rose from my chair. "I can't believe I'm doing this," I muttered. I went to

130

the bedroom, tugged my guitar case out from under the bed and carried it back out into the living room. I put it down next to my chair and sat.

"Okay, listen," I said. "If I'm going to play, I get to ask you a question."

Willa's eyes widened.

"Why don't you talk?" I asked. She shrugged and looked down, but I kept going. "No, I'm serious. I'm not making fun of you. I really want to know."

She rested her palms flat on the table and studied them. She took three very deep breaths and whispered, "It's hard."

"Talking? Why?"

She shook her head and wrote in her notebook.

It's called selective mutism. I want to talk but words won't come out.

I got stuck on two of the words. "What does this say?" I asked, pointing.

She sighed and looked at her hands. After a few beats, I heard her small voice. "Selective mutism."

"Oh," I said. I felt bad for making her say it, but she didn't look embarrassed. "But how come you could talk at your house?"

She shrugged and looked down, tapping her fingers on her notebook. Then she wrote.

It's safe there.

She shrugged again, and her expression told me there wasn't anything else to say.

I didn't really understand, but I didn't need to push her. I pulled my guitar case up to my lap. Popping it open, I said, "Just so you know, I never play in front of anyone."

She smiled, tapping her head like she was having a thought. Then she stood and walked into the kitchen, standing with her back to me.

I snorted and lifted the guitar to rest on my leg. Without giving myself time to think too hard about it, I placed my fingers on the strings and started to play.

When I was finished, she returned to the table clapping loudly. Then she pointed to her question again.

Where do you go?

"I wasn't really thinking about anything," I said. "I just sort of, I don't know, float up out of myself. Like I don't have to worry about anything."

She nodded, smiling. "Poetry," she whispered.

Just then Marcus pushed through the front door. "Hey, now, what's going on here?" He dropped his stuff next to mine in the entryway and sauntered over to the table, slapping my back harder than necessary.

"Uh, this is Willa, from my Language Arts class," I stuttered. I was afraid Marcus was going to tease or otherwise embarrass me.

"I'm Marcus, Sam's much older, much wiser, and much more handsome brother." Marcus pulled his hand from my back and extended it to Willa, who shook it with a grin. "Nice to meet you, Willa," Marcus released her hand and headed into the kitchen. I breathed a sigh of relief.

Moments later Mom walked in balancing grease-stained bags with her purse and files. I jumped up to help her and introduced Willa as I took the bags to the kitchen. Marcus was standing by the sink chugging milk straight out of the carton. He turned and grinned at me, his top lip shiny. "Sam's got a girlfr—" he began.

"NO," I broke in. "She's a friend, and she's helping me with an assignment."

"Uh-huh," Marcus winked. "I see you got the guitar out."

I punched him in the arm. "Like I said, she's helping me with an assignment. She is just my friend."

"Okay, okay," said Marcus, setting down the carton of milk and holding up his hands. "I was just kidding."

"It's not funny," I muttered.

"Hi boys," Mom said, entering the kitchen. "Sam, I've invited Willa to stay for dinner. I told her I always buy an extra hamburger with you two around." She kissed us each on the cheek. "Marcus, will you pour drinks for us?"

I glanced out at the table, but Willa wasn't there. "Where'd she go? Did you scare her away?"

Mom laughed. "Bathroom. I pointed it out for her." She lowered her voice as Marcus stuck his head into the refrigerator. "I talked to your Language Arts teacher today, Ms…"

"Abaroa," I said, when she hesitated.

"Right," she said. "We have a meeting scheduled for next week after school. She wants you there, too."

I shrugged.

"It sounds like she really cares about you," Mom whispered as Marcus approached. Then she raised her voice to normal. "So Marcus, how was your…"

She was interrupted by pounding on the front door.

Chaos

We looked at each other quizzically.

More pounding. Mom went to the door and looked through the peephole, then turned to face us. Her face was drained of color. "It's your father," she said shakily. She reached for the doorknob.

"Mom, stop." Marcus took a step forward. "Is he drunk?" His voice was low and controlled.

"I think so," Mom whispered.

"Stand back with Sam," Marcus ordered, and surprisingly Mom didn't argue. She walked back toward me, looking smaller than she had five minutes ago. "Dad," Marcus said loudly to the door. "Dad, go home and sleep it off."

"I just want to talk," Dad's voice was muffled and slurring. "Please, I just want to talk."

"Marcus," Mom said quietly. "Let him in."

"No. Not like this."

Dad thumped on the door again, less firmly this time. "Please..." his voice whined.

"Marcus..." Mom begged. "We can't leave him out there."

"Yes we can," Marcus grumbled, but he opened the door and filled the doorway with his large frame.

"Hi, son," I heard Dad say.

"What do you want?" Marcus asked. He stood like an offensive lineman, legs wide and back arched.

Dad pushed past Marcus before Marcus could resist. I heard Mom gasp and stiffen beside me.

"Please," Dad said, stumbling toward Mom, "Jenny, I just want to talk."

"Not when you're drunk," Mom said. "I told you."

Dad kept moving toward Mom. "Jenny…"

I stepped between them.

Dad tried to juke past me as he had done with Marcus at the door, but his momentum swung him off-balance and he stumbled. Marcus grabbed his arm. "Let's go, Dad," he said.

"I'm not leaving without you guys," he shouted. "You need to come home!" He tried unsuccessfully to jerk his arm out of Marcus's grasp. His voice became a wail. "You all need to come home!"

Suddenly, the room was in chaos. We were all shouting. Dad struggled to get out of Marcus's grasp. Mom tried to get around me to

136

yell at Dad. I moved side to side to keep Mom from getting too close to him, and Marcus pulled Dad toward the door.

The slam of the bathroom door stunned us into silence.

I looked over Mom's shoulder at Willa. She stood at the opening of the hallway with her fists clenched at her sides and her face twisted with alarm.

None of us spoke. I turned from Willa and looked at Dad. He stopped resisting Marcus, who loosened his grip until his hands fell to his sides. Dad looked at each of us, tears welling in his eyes. Then he looked down at his feet.

"I'm sorry," he whispered. "I'm so sorry."

"Get help or don't come back," Marcus growled. He seemed to grow a few inches as he looked down at Dad.

Still looking at his feet, Dad shuffled to the door and let himself out.

We stood there for what seemed like forever, our heavy breathing slowing back to normal, blinking as if we had just stepped into the sunlight. Willa moved first. She pulled her backpack from the chair and quietly set her notebook and pencil inside. She took out her phone and sent a quick text, then stuck her phone in the backpack also. The *zip* shot through the room and jolted me out of my daze.

"Oh, honey, you don't have to go," Mom said weakly. "I'm so sorry. Please stay for dinner."

Willa shook her head. As she passed me, she gave me a weak but kind smile. *It's okay*, her eyes said. "See ya," I choked, my eyes filling against my will.

Just as her hand touched the doorknob, there was a knock. We all jumped. "Hey, y'all in there?" Gus's muffled voice filled the room like a warm blanket. Mom nodded, and Willa opened the door.

"Oh, hi there," said Gus, taking his hat off and giving Willa a slight bow. He looked past her into our living room. "Ms. Jenny, everything okay? I heard some yellin'."

Mom looked at us, then exhaled as if she'd been holding her breath for months. "Oh, Gus, you're so kind. We're okay. Come in." Her voice shook.

Gus and Willa slid past each other in the doorway. Gus and Mom sat together on the couch and talked in low voices. Marcus wiped his eyes and patted me on the shoulder on his way to the bedroom. I stood where I was, my eyes on Willa. She looked at me as she pulled the door shut.

It's okay.

< Messages
Dad
Contact
What's wrong? Are you okay?
I'm fine, just needed to leave. Will explain later. Meet me on the corner?
Be there in 10 minutes
Thanks.
I love you Dad.

DECEMBER

Recovery

Mom pulled the car into the parking lot. A sandwich board on the sidewalk by the restaurant door advertised Happy Hour specials of two-for-one hot wings and half-priced nachos. Neither Marcus nor I made a move to get out of the car.

"You guys okay?" Mom asked, looking at Marcus next to her before turning to peer at me in the back seat. "You still up for this?"

We remained silent. I looked back at the Happy Hour sign. A dancing frog held a steaming plate of food above his head.

"Listen, you don't have to go in if you don't want to. But personally I think you should. Your dad wants to make things right." She sighed. "And so do I. We've both made mistakes here. I admit that."

"He's the drunk," Marcus muttered.

"Yes, that's true," Mom nodded. "But I didn't recognize how much he was struggling until it was too late. I didn't help him the way I might have. I just got mad." She looked at each of us again, this time more pointedly. "And I know I didn't talk through it enough with you guys. I just expected you to go along with everything." She inhaled, then let out a longer sigh than I'd ever heard. "I'm really sorry. For everything this past year."

The car was quiet for a minute or two. Then Marcus unbuckled his seatbelt, leaned over and gave Mom a kiss on the cheek.

"See you in an hour," he said. "C'mon, little man." He pushed the car door open with his shoulder, climbed out and shut the door.

My throat tightened and my eyes grew wet. I still didn't move.

She turned as far around as she could in order to face me. "Sam, you are one of the strongest kids I know."

"No, I'm not," I blurted. "I don't ever know what to do."

"What are you talking about?" Her eyebrows raised. "You always know what to do."

"No, I don't," I retorted. "I just do what you expect me to do."

She hesitated before speaking again, and when she did she chose her words carefully. "Sam, part of growing up is figuring out how to balance what you want with what other people want from you. It's okay if you haven't completely gotten there yet. Most of us haven't."

I must have looked really confused, because she laughed quietly. She reached back and put her hand on my knee.

"Trust me, kiddo. You can do anything."

I wiped my eyes with the back of my hand and sniffed, then sat up just a little bit taller. "Love you, Mom," I said, speaking each word clearly. I put my hand on the door handle.

"I love you too, Sam," she replied. "See you in an hour."

The day after Dad had stormed our apartment, I came home from school to find Mom on the couch. Her eyes were red and puffy and she had never looked so tired. But some of the worry lines that had crossed her forehead for months seemed less deep, and there was a light in her eyes that I hadn't seen since we'd moved. She told me that she and Dad had agreed to see a counselor, but first Dad was going into treatment for his drinking. She didn't promise anything, and I knew she couldn't. But for the first time in months, I felt like maybe life was going to move forward.

Dad completed a short inpatient detox program, which meant he stayed there until he was sober. Kind of like a hospital, is what

144

Mom said. Now he attended daily recovery meetings, and he and Mom were in therapy together. Mom said that she couldn't promise us that we would move back home, but she could promise that she and Dad were both dedicated to being good parents to us.

Dad had chosen the restaurant, a place we'd never been between Lyndale and our new town. We walked in. A waitress greeted us at the door, her wide body straining the brown embroidered uniform. She waved her long nails and gave a hearty "Hi folks! Two for lunch?"

"We're meeting someone," Marcus said as our eyes scanned both sides of the restaurant. He tapped my arm and I looked in the direction he gestured with his chin.

Dad sat in a booth, looking smaller and older than the last time we'd seen him. His thick coat was wrapped around him, collar up. A mug sat in front of him on the table. As we walked toward him, he sat up taller, then slid out of the booth and rose as we approached. He reached out his hand, then pulled it back.

"Hi, guys," he said as we all settled into the booth. Marcus and I filled one side, sitting so close that our shoulders were touching.

"Hi Dad," we said, almost in unison.

"Okay, folks, what'll it be? Sodas? Lemonade?" The waitress had arrived at our tableside, her large voice filling the awkward space. Marcus and I ordered drinks, and she left.

"Thanks for coming," Dad said. His words were careful, as though they were landing on thin glass. I heard a slight quiver in his voice. "I wasn't sure if you'd want to."

We didn't say anything. He looked down at his hands as they folded and unfolded on the table. "I know this has been hard on you…"

Hard on us? Having to move, adjust to a new school, watching Mom stressing out, remembering everything…

I was suddenly furious. The words flew out before I had time to think.

"How do *you* know how it's been?" I asked. I felt Marcus turn and look at me, but I kept going. "How do *you* know how hard this has been for us? You just disappeared! First you disappeared by drinking, and then we just didn't see you!"

Dad was nodding, his eyes trained on the table. Marcus was still looking at me. I was saying things I didn't even know I was thinking.

"You always tell us never to give up, to go for what we want," I continued. "But you just gave up! Why? Just because you lost a job?"

Dad was still nodding. Marcus nudged my leg with his under the table. I noticed that tears trickled down Dad's cheeks, and my anger softened.

Just then the waitress came back with our drinks. "Here you go, boys...oh." She stopped and whispered, "I'll give y'all a minute" before quickly walking away.

Dad wiped his cheeks with a napkin and unceremoniously blew his nose. Then he looked up at us, his eyelids drooping with fatigue. He took a deep breath.

"I have a lot to make up for with the two of you," he said quietly. "I know I have hurt you. I know I've lost your trust. But right now, I am promising you..." He paused, sitting up a little straighter and looking us each straight in the eye. "I am promising you," he repeated, "that I am going to earn back your trust. You two are the most important people in my life. I am going to get better. It's all very complicated and it will take a long time, but I am going to stay sober. I am going to be there for you. It won't look the same as before, but I will be a better father. I promise." Then he sank back against the seat, as though that speech had taken every drop of energy out of him. "I love you boys."

"We know, Dad," Marcus said. He reached across the table and patted Dad's folded hands. "We know."

Dad's eyes filled again. He looked at me, and I nodded.

Friends

Willa and I never mentioned the night at my apartment when Dad barged in. The morning after it happened, she smiled that kind smile again. She didn't look at me with pity, which I appreciated. It was more like she was glad to know me better.

We ate lunch together that day, and every day from then on. She always brought her notebook so that we could have conversations. One day, Jose joined us. Another day, two girls from Willa's science class sat with us. But whether or not anyone else joined us, we could count on each other.

Willa invited me to go to the open mic with her and her dad again. I agreed to meet them there, and I even brought my guitar. But at the last minute I chickened out and didn't sign up. Willa didn't, either, even though her dad still seemed confident that someday she would.

At the frozen yogurt shop afterwards, Willa's dad brought up guitar lessons.

"Have you ever taken them?" he asked.

"No," I replied shyly. I was reminded of the conversation with Dad about this very topic, and I cleared my throat. "No, I haven't," I repeated.

"Well, it just so happens that I know a guy," Willa's dad said. He proceeded to tell me that a man he worked with taught guitar lessons on the side. "So, if you're interested, I could give you his number."

"Um, I…I don't…maybe," I stuttered. I looked at Willa, who had a grin on her face. "Well, yeah, um, okay."

"Great!" he said. "I'll find it at home and send it with Willa tomorrow."

So maybe I'll take guitar lessons.

Winner Winner

Ms. Abaroa announced to the class that despite some of our less-than-enthusiastic attitudes about entering the poetry competition, we actually had a winner in our midst.

"Willa's poem won your age category! Let's give her a round of applause," Ms. Abaroa cheered. I jerked up from my slouch and turned to look at Willa. A smile was creeping across her face, but she didn't look up. Her cheeks flushed behind her hair.

"Winner winner chicken dinner!" Max hooted from his seat in the front row as the applause died down. Laughter bubbled up around the room.

"Thanks for that, Max," Ms. Abaroa rolled her eyes and shook her head. "And I hope to see all of you at the celebration next Thursday evening."

Once the class settled into the day's work, Ms. Abaroa came over and sat backward in the seat in front of Willa. "So, they're expecting you to read your poem at the event," she said quietly. "What do you think?"

Willa shrugged.

"I can ask the coordinator of the event if it's okay that you don't read," Ms. Abaroa said.

"I'm sure it would be fine. Or maybe someone can read it in your place."

Willa looked up. "I want to," she whispered. Her eyes sparkled.

Ms. Abaroa couldn't hide her surprise. Then her face relaxed into a smile. "Alright," she said. "But if you change your mind…" She rose. "I'm proud of you, Willa."

Willa smiled and looked back down at her notebook. Without lifting her head, she shot me a look from the corner of her eyes. *What?*

I grinned. "Nothing," I replied.

A Little Help

Marcus and I cut through the dark high school parking lot and entered the Commons. The bright light stung my eyes. People filled the cavernous room, their voices hushed as they moved from one display to the next as if they were afraid of disturbing the words. Marcus elbowed me in the ribs and pointed up at a sign hanging from the ceiling. *Poets 17-and-under*. We wove our way through the crowd, trying not to hip-check anyone bent over to read a poem.

Tables lined with tri-fold poster boards made a two-layer square around the room. In the center of the square, folding chairs were set in rows facing a podium. Each board had eight poems on each side.

Ms. Abaroa had said that there would be a lot of submissions, but there were way more than I expected. There were dozens of poems just written by kids. Other teachers must have required it too, I figured. I still couldn't imagine that many kids sitting around writing poetry *just because*.

Marcus seemed surprisingly interested in the poetry. He bent over with his hands on his thighs to read a poem at waist level. It was

Jose's poem about spaghetti. He laughed out loud. "Nice," he muttered. Then he remembered me. "Hey, where's yours?"

We searched for a minute or two until we found my poem. It was in the top left corner of a board. I didn't recognize the names of kids next to or below it. I'd written the poem about Dad. It was filled with unanswered questions, but I'd felt pounds lighter after I'd put it on paper. Ms. Abaroa had helped me correct the spelling of almost every word, of course, but I was proud of how it turned out. As Marcus read it, his expression stayed neutral. Then he looked at me for a long moment, as if trying to dig through my eyes and pull out what was buried inside.

"It's good," he said. "You should show it to Mom when she gets here."

"Yeah, maybe," I said.

"You should," he repeated.

"Okay then."

"Okay then." He grinned and punched me in the arm.

Willa stood with her parents as they chatted with Ms. Abaroa. Her hair was pulled back in a rubber band and she was wearing a yellow dress with her purple Converse. She studied the floor intently.

"I'll be right back," I said to Marcus.

"Uh-huh," he grunted as he read another poem.

Willa glanced up as I got closer and she grinned. *I'm glad you're here.* She tipped her head back toward the floor. I stood next to her, looking for the spot she was staring at.

"Hey," I said.

After a slow beat she responded quietly. "Hey."

Ms. Abaroa noticed me then. "Sam! I'm so glad you came!" she exclaimed. "Is your mom here?" Her eyebrows lifted with expectation. "I so enjoyed talking with her the other day."

The meeting between my mom and Ms. Abaroa had been relatively painless. Ms. Abaroa explained that I had some dyslexic tendencies and what that meant. She told me I would in fact have to start an intensive reading class in the next semester. She also suggested a lot of strategies, including listening to audiobooks. When I'd asked if that was cheating, she'd laughed. "Remember the three-legged dog," she'd teased, but her eyes were kind.

"No, my mom's at work," I said, my voice loud over the noise of the growing crowd. "She's meeting us here. My brother and I walked over." I gestured to where Marcus stood, now talking to a high school girl. Of course. She giggled at whatever he said, and he preened like a peacock.

"Well, I'm glad you're here," Ms. Abaroa repeated.

Willa's dad clapped me on the shoulder. "Sam, buddy, how the heck are you?" He always seemed so happy to see me. He turned to the woman next to him, who I assumed was Willa's mom. "Honey, this is Willa's friend Sam. He moved here from Lyndale this fall."

"Hello, Sam," she said in a soft voice, reaching out her hand to shake mine. "It's really nice to meet you. Willa's told me a lot about you." She beamed at me, and I felt my face get hot.

I glanced at Willa and saw that she was still looking at the floor, but now her cheeks were pink. I couldn't picture her talking to her mom about me, but I guess she had.

"Nice to meet you, too," I replied. Willa's mom held onto my hand for a bit longer than was comfortable, then released it. She kept smiling at me. It was an open, *I've never been*

156

more thrilled smile. I felt like I was sitting in a patch of sunlight on the floor like Willa's cat.

Jack appeared out of nowhere. "Mom, guess what? Oh, hey Sam. Mom guess what? There's a poem over there about boogers. Isn't that so crazy? Willa, I found your poem—it's on the wall by the door. I saw Brian over there, can I sit with him? Okay, thanks." Without waiting for a response, he was off. "Brian! Hey, BRIAN!"

Willa's dad smiled at his wife. "I'm on it," he said, moving toward the trail Jack had blazed through the crowd.

Willa's mom was still smiling at me. Her eyes were weirdly shiny, almost like they held tears. I gave her what I hoped looked like a polite smile instead of an incredibly awkward grimace.

"Um, I need to go find my brother," I said. "Good luck," I added quietly to Willa. She looked at me from the corners of her eyes. Her mouth opened slightly. I saw an *I don't know about this* expression flicker across her flushed face. Without thinking I grabbed her hand and squeezed it. Then I headed toward Marcus, who was helping himself to a cookie.

A voice over the microphone asked us to head to our seats. A grandfatherly man stood at the podium, looking pleased with the crowd as we merged like cattle into the rows of folding chairs. So much like cattle, in fact, that Marcus couldn't resist.

"Mooooooo," he said. A few people around us chuckled.

As the man at the mic talked about sponsors and the origins of the contest, I looked around the room. At least a couple hundred people were there. Willa and her parents sat in the front row with people I assumed were the other winners. I counted ten kids from class from where I was sitting. Jose and Max lingered by the platters of cookies. Xavier sat with his family while Ashley and her friends hunched together whispering as usual.

"This year's competition had the most submissions we've ever seen in all categories. Choosing the winners out of so many amazing writers was no easy task for the committee." He paused and cleared his throat, the sticky sound echoing through the microphone. "But we unanimously agreed on all of our winning poems. So let's hear them!"

A burst of applause and cheers rang out through the room. The man looked pleased, soaking it in as if it was intended for him. He smoothed his comb-over with his palm and smiled out at the audience.

"We will start with the winner in the 11-and-under category…"

A boy who looked to be about Jack's age stood up from the front row and walked to the podium. I could see from where I sat that he was a bundle of nerves. Avoiding eye contact with the audience, he read his poem so fast that I missed some of the words. His poem was about his dead dog. But somehow the writing was filled with joy and happy memories. I thought about asking him how he did that.

"Wonderful, just wonderful," the emcee murmured into the microphone as the boy sat down. I watched as his parents leaned into him from each side, rubbing his shoulders and beaming.

"Next, in our 12-to-18 category, a poem by Willa Vaughn."

A smattering of applause rippled across the audience as Willa stood from her seat in the front row and made her way to the podium. I heard quiet voices and I turned. Ashley was smirking and shaking her head. I stared lasers at her until she met my eyes. Surprisingly, her face changed from sneering to almost sad. She looked away.

Willa stepped behind the podium. She stared at her poem and chewed her lip. Then she lifted her head and looked at her parents. Her mom leaned forward in her seat. It looked from behind like her mom was saying something, but I couldn't hear her voice. Willa nodded and looked back at her poem. The audience shifted uncomfortably.

I could tell that her words were trying to come out. She took in a short breath and opened her mouth, then closed it again. She did this several times before looking at her parents again, pleading. Her forehead creased; tears weren't far behind.

She was giving up.

Her dad sat on the edge of his chair. He looked like he would stand at any moment.

Someone in the audience coughed as I squeezed out of my row and made my way up to the front. By the time I was standing next to Willa, a quiet murmur rolled through the crowd.

"Look," I whispered into her ear. "You can read it or I will. I'll stand here or I can leave if you want. But you've got this."

Her eyes were wide and filled with terror as they searched mine. Then her face relaxed a little and she grinned her *you're a jerk* grin, her lips pursed and lifted on one side. Only it was different this time. Her eyes were telling a story, one about the many times that she couldn't talk and the disappointment that came after. She blinked slowly, then looked back at me. She pointed to the first word with a purple fingernail.

"Together?" I whispered. She nodded. We leaned into the microphone side by side, our shoulders touching. With familiar dread I looked at the page resting on the podium, but to my surprise the letters stopped shifting and settled into place. I guessed those words knew they shouldn't stand in Willa's way.

We started reading. Her voice was barely a whisper. I'm sure the audience only heard me.

We hold words on a stem
like dandelion seeds

I stumbled over the word *dandelion*. Her voice kept going.

where the simplest puff
releases them to ride the wind.

161

With each word, her voice became more clear, stronger, and kind of musical. I stopped reading but continued to look at the page. I was afraid to move.

we draw words
from our deepest roots

She read quickly but with expression, her voice rising and falling with the cadence of the poem.

expose them to the air,
where they flower, seed,
and return to the earth.

I held my breath. We stood as still as statues.

A thousand words
in a picture we
paint with each breath;
thick with the truth of
who we are.
wait... listen...

And then she was finished. The audience burst into applause. I looked at her parents. They were both crying. So was Ms. Abaroa.

Willa and I pulled our shoulders apart and looked at each other. She still had that *you're a jerk* grin, but there was more. Her eyes shone.

"Thanks," she whispered, and her eyes drifted back to the floor.

"Anytime," I whispered back, and I went back to my seat so she could enjoy her moment. As I did, I saw Mom standing in the back. She had both hands over her heart and tears on her cheeks. She smiled at me, and I smiled back.

The rest of the evening went on with a handful of adult winners reading poems. To be honest, I didn't really listen to them. I watched Willa's back, her parents' arms wrapped around her from both sides, and tried to keep from thinking about the fact that I had just read aloud in public.

When the poets were finished, the crowd mingled over cookies while the winners stood together for a photo op. Willa and the boy who read first looked like uncomfortable kids at a family reunion, surrounded by adults and anxious to race off. They both shifted their weight until the photographer finally released the group.

"That was pretty cool, what you did." Marcus stood next to me, his low voice barely audible over the crowd. "So, is she your…"

"No," I interrupted. "God. Why do you always…"

"Just asking!" Marcus grinned, raising his hands in defense. "I'm getting another cookie. Want one?"

I shook my head and watched Willa as kids from our class filed past her. I only caught a few words.

"That was so…"

"I liked your…"

"Great job…"

"I've never heard you…"

She looked equal parts embarrassed, uncomfortable, proud and happy. She said nothing and held her head high, even though her gaze remained pulled to the floor. People patted her shoulders and stood way too close. I wanted to tell them to give her space, but I didn't. I imagined her as a willow tree, strong roots reaching deep into the soil, flexible trunk swaying gently.

She didn't need saving.

Ashley held back, uncharacteristically waiting until there was no audience of friends for her to perform for. Her expression was unlike anything I'd seen on her. It almost looked... friendly. I couldn't hear her voice as she spoke to Willa.

I watched Willa's mouth form the words— "No thanks"—before she turned toward her parents and let herself be swallowed by their embraces.

Ashley looked around and our eyes connected. We stayed like that for a long second, and I watched her face shift from humane to steel. She shrugged, narrowed her eyes, and looked away.

I turned to find Marcus. He was talking to the high school girl again. It looked like phone numbers were being exchanged. I looked for Mom. She stood by the door, chatting with another woman.

"You are a good man, Sam Ward." I turned. Ms. Abaroa stood in front of me. Her serious face broke into a broad smile. "Willa is lucky to have you as a friend."

"Yeah, well..." I stammered, then let my voice trail off. I wasn't sure what to say to that.

Ms. Abaroa's face became serious again. "That must have been hard for you. To think about reading that poem in front of everyone."

"I didn't even think about it. I just did it," I replied.

"Well, maybe that's the Golden Ticket," she said, and grinned as she put her hand on my arm. "Let's talk more about that during school. I have some ideas." She winked. "I'll see you tomorrow."

"See you tomorrow," I repeated. As much as I wasn't looking forward to hearing her ideas about reading, I had a feeling she genuinely wanted to help me.

And maybe it was okay to need a little help.

EPILOGUE

OMG! That video was amazing! I'm so proud of you!!!!!!!!!!!!

Thanks!

Was that Sam up there with you?

Yep!

I'm so glad you have a mid-winter break in February. I can't wait to visit you!

Open mic?

Totally! Yogurt after?

You know it!

The open mic host stepped behind the mic and boomed a five-minute warning to the crowd. He ran his hand through his curly hair and smoothed his shirt over his broad torso. On the front, a triangle said *"You're pointless"* to a sad-looking circle. I rolled my eyes and turned to Marcus, seated beside me at the small table with a cup of coffee in front of him.

"Since when do you drink coffee?" I asked.

He shrugged and puffed out his chest. "Since now, who cares?"

Mom poked him in the arm. "Drink that and you'll be up all night, big man."

"Yeah, yeah," Marcus grinned. He never minded being teased.

"Is he really coming?" I asked Mom.

"That's what he said," she answered, nodding. "He was very excited." She paused. "He's working so hard at sobriety, and he really wants to do right by you guys. By all of us."

Neither Marcus nor I said anything. It had been a couple of months since we'd seen Dad at the restaurant, and we'd only talked to him on the phone a few times. He didn't really talk about his recovery, but Mom said he was doing pretty well. She still saw him every week for therapy.

I felt a tap on my shoulder and turned around. Willa and her dad were standing behind me, along with another girl I didn't recognize. Willa's dad clapped his hand on my shoulder as usual and then shook hands with Mom and Marcus.

Willa smiled, but no words came. The other girl leaned in front of her.

"I'm Sarah," she said. "You must be Sam."

I nodded. "Hey."

"I used to live here," she said. "I'm just visiting until tomorrow."

I looked at Willa. She looked as content as I had ever seen her, like everything was right with the world. She looked at me and grinned.

"You play?" Sarah asked, pointing at my guitar.

"Yep, I'm going to play tonight." My heart rose into my throat at the thought.

I heard Willa gasp. I looked at her, and she raised her hand for a high-five. *Yes!* her expression said.

"Break a leg, Sam!" Willa's dad beamed, steering the girls toward an empty table. "Frozen yogurt afterwards if you all are up for it!"

"Sounds fun!" said Mom.

The open mic host walked back behind the microphone. "Okay, folks, let's get this thing going. First up, we have a guitar solo by Sam."

My heart threatened to beat out of my chest as I rose from my seat. Marcus whooped and hollered as Mom clapped faster and louder than I thought possible. I carried my guitar case up to the mic and set it on the floor, popping it open without looking up. As I stood and lifted the strap over my head, I saw Dad.

He was standing in the back, looking around. His hands were shoved in his coat pockets and his shoulders were slumped forward, like he was trying to hide inside of himself. He looked toward the place where I stood, and our eyes locked. His back straightened. He gave me a shy wave, which I returned.

"Yeah, Sam!" I heard Marcus call, and I realized I was standing in front of the microphone doing nothing. I cleared my throat, and the microphone sent the sound bouncing around the room. My heart was racing.

I looked back where Dad had been, and he was gone. I scanned the room and saw him moving toward Mom and Marcus, without taking his tired eyes off me. I smiled nervously, then scanned the room again, landing on Willa. She gave me two thumbs up and a look that said *You've got this!*

I looked down at my fingers frozen on the guitar strings. You've got this, I told myself. And I began to play.

RESOURCES

Selective Mutism

Selective Mutism is a complex childhood anxiety disorder characterized by a child's inability to speak and communicate effectively in select social settings, such as school. These children are able to speak and communicate in settings where they are comfortable, secure, and relaxed. More than 90% of children with Selective Mutism also have social phobia or social anxiety.

Selective Mutism Center

To learn more and find support, visit these websites.

Selective Mutism Association
www.selectivemutism.org

SMart Center
www.selectivemutismcenter.org

Dyslexia

Dyslexia is a specific learning disability in reading. Kids with dyslexia have trouble reading accurately and fluently. They may also have trouble with reading comprehension, spelling, and writing. It's important to know that while dyslexia impacts learning, it's not a problem of intelligence. Kids with dyslexia are just as smart as their peers.

Understood.org

To learn more and find support, visit these websites.

International Dyslexia Association
www.dyslexiaida.org

Understood
www.understood.org

Learning Ally
www.learningally.org

Acknowledgements

I have always loved reading contemporary middle grade fiction. I am endlessly inspired by authors who address realistic and often difficult topics with grace and compassion. Names that come to mind include Kate DiCamillo, Jacqueline Woodson, Sharon Creech, Jerry Spinelli, Laurie Halse Anderson, Kwame Alexander, Cythnia Lord. While these are just a few of the many authors whom I've loved since forever, they are the ones who have inspired me the most.

Publishing a book independently is by no means a solo effort. Endless thanks to the Village Books Publishing team for the enthusiastic support and go-betweening that made this book possible. Thanks also to cover designer Gabi Gonzalez-Yoxtheimer for reading my mind and designing the perfect images, and interior designer David Beaumier for turning my Word document into something beautiful. Amy Betz gave brilliant and invaluable editorial feedback at early and late stages of this story, and I am so grateful.

I cannot thank enough the people in my personal life who championed this book. Early readers Lisa, Jackie, Colleen, Meredith, and Dawn, thank you for your friendship and candid feedback. Willa, Sam and I are all better people because of you. Kiersten, thank you for the insight into dyslexia and enthusiasm for these characters. My writing group – Jackie, Blanche, Colleen, Carol and Kate – I am a more honest writer and human because of our community.

I taught elementary education for many years and was challenged and inspired by each and every one of my students. I am proud of you and will always be in your corner.

My extended family: Marc, Jane, Caleb, Connor, and Tom – I wouldn't be me without you. Mom, thank you for teaching me to really *see* people. And, you know, for being my mom. I love you.

And, finally, the three loves of my life. Mark, thank you for your unwavering support in the face of all the wild ideas I have. You never fail to believe in my ability to pull them off, even when I doubt myself. This wouldn't have been possible without you.

Eva and Jacob, I love you both more than chocolate. This book is for you.

Stephanie Dethlefs is a writer and story coach. She spent over a decade teaching elementary school. *Unspoken* is her first book. Stephanie lives in Pacific Northwest Washington with her husband, daughter and son and loves playing outside and curling up with a good book.

www.StephanieDethlefs.com

. CPSIA information can be obtained
at www.ICGtesting.com
Printed in the USA
LVHW080217170220
647156LV00015B/472

9 780578 499130